The Craigslist Incident

Jason Fisk

Published by Unsolicited Press.
First Edition.

The Craigslist Incident is a work of fiction and a product of the author's imagination. Any resemblance in this novel to actual events or persons, living or dead, is entirely coincidental.

Attention schools and businesses: for discounted copies on large orders, please contact the publisher directly.

For information contact:
Unsolicited Press
Portland, Oregon
www.unsolicitedpress.com
orders@unsolicitedpress.com
619-354-8005

Cover Design: Kathryn Gerhardt
Editor: Kristen Marckmann

To Laura, Delia, Jonas, and Ezra with love

Posted 10 days ago

Women Seeking Men: I'm an 18-year-old female and I want to take a hit out on myself.

The Reply:
From: Joe Dolsen
To: Craigslist Ad: Women Seeking Men

Hey… Obviously, I'm responding to your ad on Craigslist. WTF? You want to take a hit out on yourself? I'm not saying NO, but I have been depressed and through some shit, too, if you want to talk before you do anything drastic. My name is Joe Dolsen. I'm 20 and not married – not that that matters – just want to help if I can. Email me: joeblackout3117@gmail.com.

Edna Barrett

When Edna was young, she thought her family was happy. Her father used to say that she was an exact copy of him. That delighted her. She loved her father more than anything she had ever loved. She tried to go with him whenever and wherever she could. On this occasion, she'd managed to be in his pickup truck driving along Highway Seven. The warm morning air passed freely through the open window, whipping her hair around her freckled eight-year-old face. They drove past a group of hunters who were loading up their camouflage flat-bottomed boat with oversized bags of duck hunting gear.

"You know why I don't hunt anymore?" he asked. She shook her head. "I quit hunting when I got serious about your mother." He looked over at Edna who had squared herself into the corner of the seat, angling away from the wind so she could hear his words. She squinted and nodded; errant wisps of hair flying wildly around her face.

"With her being a veterinarian tech and everything, and my loving her so much, it only made sense. You know, it broke my heart, seeing her face every time I brought home a dead duck. Good God, she really hated it when I killed deer."

"That's why we're hunting with your camera now, right?" she asked, being well versed in this part of the story. "So you don't have to kill animals, right?"

"That's right," he said and turned into the Carver County Forest Preserve. He put the old Chevy in park, and they climbed out and walked to the back of the truck. He lowered the tailgate and pulled out his green canvas bag filled with a camera, film, and other picture taking accoutrements. "You're going to have to watch where you step, and make sure you don't make any noise."

"I'm so excited," she said and clasped her hands.

"I've got a little surprise for you," he said as he dug around in his bag.

"You do! What is it? What is it?"

"I thought you might want to snap some pictures, too," he said and handed her a green and white disposable camera. "You press this button to take the photo. Every time you take one, you'll have to advance the film here, like this. Roll it to the right. Got it?"

"I get it," she said, taking the camera and looking through the viewfinder. She snapped a picture of a tree.

"Now, be careful 'cause you can only take twenty-four pictures with that camera. Well, twenty-three now, so you'd best make 'em all count."

"Okay," she said, examining the camera. She took a picture of her father's back as he bent over the truck. "That one counted," she said and smiled.

"I hope my backside didn't crack your lens," he said as he put the strap around his neck and snugged the bag over his shoulder. "Let's go hunting," he said.

They spent the entire morning hiking through the forest preserve, taking pictures of nature. Her dad liked to take pictures of all sorts of birds in trees and on the ground. Edna spaced out her pictures and had one left when they got back in the truck to go home. "Hey dad," she said while he was driving.

"Yeah," he said, looking from the road to her.

"I've got one picture left," she said and smiled. He smiled back at her. She snapped the picture right at that moment. "Oh, that one is going to be good! Can we get these developed today?"

"We can drop 'em off, but we can't wait around to pick them up," he said. "We'll have to get 'em tomorrow or something."

"I'm so excited. That last picture was a good one," she said and smiled.

Two days later, her father walked into the house and handed her a black and yellow envelope filled with the photos she had taken on the hike. She sat down on the couch and opened the envelope. "Look at these with me," she told her dad and scooted over to make room for him on the couch. He plopped down beside her; his weight caused her to lean into him. She didn't mind. She thumbed through the pictures, smiling at the shots of birds and squirrels she had taken. She hurried through the stack, looking for the picture of her father she had taken in the truck. It was the last picture in the pile. She went silent as she stared at the picture. It was a picture of her thumb. Tears welled in her eyes, waiting to fall. Her father laughed.

"What? That's not funny," she said. "It's a picture of my thumb."

"Come one. You gotta laugh at that. You thought you'd taken a great picture of me and come to find out it's a great picture of your thumb," he said. "Besides, it's the only picture of me that I really like," he said and smiled at her.

"Ha-ha," she said sarcastically. He put his arm around her and gave her a hug.

A terrible accident

"Mom," Edna said, as she sluggishly walked down the stairs of the creaky old house.

"What?" her mother asked, looking up from her breakfast. She looked like an angel with the summer sun bursting through window behind her, enveloping her in light.

"I don't want you guys to get a divorce," Edna said as she sat down at the table.

"You heard us last night?" her mom asked, putting her coffee cup on the table.

"Um, I'm pretty sure that the entire neighborhood heard you guys last night." She grabbed the Wheaties box and poured herself a bowl. "You two were loud."

"Well, sometimes that's what adults do," Edna's mother said, digging the triangle segments out of her halved grapefruit.

"Do you have to give him such a hard time? Maybe you could cut him a break every now and then."

"Edna Jean Barret," her mother said. "You have no idea what's *really* going on. If you did, you'd feel sorry for *me* and not your father."

"*So,* tell me what's going on."

"You're thirteen. Way too young to understand, and besides, this is between your father and I."

"Is he coming home?"

"He just went for a hike. He'll be back."

"I heard him leave late last night. People don't go on hikes in the middle of the night."

"Honestly, I'm not sure where he is," her mom said and looked out the window at the driveway.

"Is he all right?" Edna asked.

"I hope so, honey," Edna's mother said. "I really hope so."

Later that afternoon, Edna was walking through the busy hallway of her junior high when she heard an announcement crackle over the loudspeaker requesting that she, Edna Barrett, go to the main office. When she got there, the secretary ushered her into a conference room. The air in the room was stuffy and held a charge like Edna had never felt before. She saw her mother and grandmother leaning into each other, knees touching under the table, hands full of tissues, both crying.

"Edna!" Her mother rose from her chair and hurried to her. They embraced, Edna's mother buried her head in the nook of her daughter's shoulder and began sobbing. Edna felt her heart sink.

"What's going on?" she asked.

"It's your father. There's been a horrible accident," her mother said lifting her head from Edna's shoulder, looking her in the eye.

"Is he okay?" Edna asked as she stepped back, assessing both women.

"I'm afraid not. He's ... he's ... gone," she said. Her words exhaled as sobs.

"Dead?" Edna asked. Her mother nodded. "How?" She found herself sinking to her knees. Tears plunged down her cheeks as she sat on the floor.

"A terrible accident..." her mother said, reaching for Edna, helping her up off the floor and guiding her to a chair. Edna's mom paused and looked to Edna's grandmother as if she were asking for help with a glance.

"A hunter accidently shot him while he was hiking," her grandmother said, finishing the sentence her mother couldn't finish, stepping up and offering her version as the official version of what happened to her son. Edna didn't know it at the time, but that conversation would be the second to last time she would ever speak to her grandma.

Don't touch the coffin

The funeral took place at the Paul-McBride Funeral Chapel in Norwood, Minnesota. It was a large white building that Edna thought looked more like an old house than a funeral home. She liked that and thought her dad would have liked it, too. The day was such a blur that Edna only remembered two things.

The first was a memory of walking up to the front of the large room that housed her father's casket. The entry had an archway that opened to padded folding seats that had been set up in four rows. In Edna's estimation, there weren't enough chairs to fill up the room. She thought there should be more chairs; her father deserved more chairs. She walked to the front of the room, the whole time, staring at the closed casket, wishing she could open it and talk to her dad for a minute before he was buried. She looked over her shoulder and saw her mother and grandma talking to the funeral director. She looked up at her dad's photo on top of his casket and reached for it, putting her hand on the casket handle for balance. She stood on her tippy toes, stretching for the photo.

"Edna!" her mother yelled. "Don't touch!" Edna jumped back. She was angry. All she wanted to do was see her dad one last time, and if she couldn't see him, the least she could was touch the coffin that housed his body. *Why is she yelling at me? He's my Dad,* she thought.

"Can I please see him?" she asked her mother.

"Edna Jean, we've been over this already. I'm sorry, but it needs to stay closed. Isn't that right?" she asked the funeral director.

"Yes," he said, staring at Edna. "We need to preserve and protect the memory of your father. The accident was serious enough to warrant a closed casket. Believe me, I know. I've been doing this for 25 years," he said and walked away. Edna's mother came over and took the picture of her father off the casket and handed it to Edna. She traced his outline and hugged the picture.

The second thing Edna remembered about that day was her grandma, her father's mother, kissing her cheek. She embraced Edna. "Goodbye," she said with a finality that scared Edna. She looked up at her grandma when she released her and saw tears streaming down her face.

"I love you, Grandma," she said.

"I love you, too," her grandma said. "You remind me so much of him that it hurts," she said. She wrapped her arms around Edna again and held her for what seemed like forever. When she let go, she kissed her cheek two more times. Edna watched her grandma walk to her car and get in. Edna waved at her as she drove away, but her grandma didn't wave back, but instead stared straight ahead as she left the parking lot.

That was the last time Edna would ever see her grandma. She never asked her mother why they never saw her again. She feared it was because she reminded her grandmother of her father.

Please leave me alone

Edna was at the Palace Drugstore with her best friend, Jenny. Edna loved the way the store seemed to hug her when she walked in. She was comforted by the sweet smell of familiarity. She smiled when she heard the intimate sound of the creaking floorboards beneath her weight. Every inch of the space in the store had something for sale. The only store in the town of 3,000 people where you could buy candy, a book, an album, a necklace, and pick up your prescription. Edna was in the back, skimming through the paperback novels and magazines while Jenny was thumbing through the records near the front of the store. Edna pulled out the latest edition of her favorite periodical, *Soldier of Fortune Magazine*. She loved the tagline: *The Journal of Professional Adventurers*. Edna never ceased to be amazed by the fact that there were people who would kill other people for money, and that it all began with a simple advertisement placed in the back of the magazine that she held in her hands. *How many people have died as a result of this magazine?* she wondered as she thumbed through its pages.

"You reading about guns?" a voice asked. Edna looked up from her magazine to see two boys she recognized as seniors from school.

"I'm just looking through this," she said and turned her back to the boys, wanting to read the magazine in peace.

They pivoted with her. One of the boys put his finger on the top of Edna's magazine and lowered it.

"Aren't you that girl whose father blew his brains out in the forest preserve?" he asked.

"Please leave me alone," Edna said. She felt a panic buzz through her body. She looked toward the front of the store at the high school kid working behind the cash register, hoping for some help. He made eye contact and then looked away.

"What's going on?" Jenny asked as she walked down the aisle and stood next to Edna. Edna exhaled relief.

"Nothing. We were just talking to your friend about her dad," one boy said. "Didn't the police find him sitting in the woods with a shot gun in his mouth?" the boy asked. "I guess his brains were blown all over the tree."

"Yeah," the second boy chimed in, "I saw the tree. There's still shit wedged between the bark. Probably his brains."

Edna gulped and said, "He was shot, yes, but it was a hunting accident." She heard herself repeating the lines that her mom had coached her to say if someone ever questioned her about her father's death. She could feel tears well in her eyes.

"He worked construction, right? Lost everything to cocaine?" Edna wiped a tear from her eye before it fell. She didn't want the boys to know that they'd gotten to her. She didn't want to cry. She stood there, frozen, waiting for her brain to catch up and tell her what to do. Then, one boy pretended to put a shot gun in his mouth and pull the trigger. He staggered backward and made a gesture that indicated that his brains had been blown everywhere.

Edna couldn't take it anymore. She dropped the magazine and took a swing at the boy. He stepped back, dodging her tiny fist. Both boys were laughing. Edna lunged toward them. Her fists clenched at her sides. Jenny stepped between and pushed Edna down the aisle away from the boys.

"Y'all had better take this outside, or I'm calling the police," the high schooler yelled from the front of the store, waving his iPhone above his head.

"Come on," Jenny said, and grabbed Edna's hand. "Let's get out of here." They marched out of the store and headed toward Jenny's house. "Those boys don't know what they're talking about," Jenny said.

"I just wish people didn't bring his death up," Edna said. She stopped to look at Jenny. "I just wanna get the fuck outta this town. I wanna go where no one knows anything about me." She began sobbing.

Jenny took Edna's hands. "Your dad loved you," she said. She pulled Edna close and hugged her.

Just then a car rounded the corner and the horn blared. One of the boys from the drug store leaned out his window and yelled, "Rent a room, lesbians!"

You're an abomination

It was just after fourth period, and Edna was waiting in line to get her lunch. The lunchroom doubled as the second school gymnasium, so it always smelled like a combination of locker room and food. She hated standing in line. She felt like a dragonfly pinned to display board. She thought everyone knew that she was getting free-and-reduced lunch because she was so poor. Her mom couldn't afford to pay for everything on a nurse's-aide income. She scanned the lunchroom and saw Jenny sitting in their normal spot, eating a sandwich and waiting for Edna. She waved. Jenny waved back.

"There she is. The lesbian," the senior from the drug store said. He stopped on the other side of the lunch line and stared at her; the hate in his eyes scared Edna.

"What do you want?" she asked.

"You think you're pretty tough, trying to hit a guy who wouldn't hit a girl back? Well I've got news for you. Don't fuck with me because I won't hesitate to punch your gay ass out. You're an abomination."

Edna turned and moved forward with the line, ignoring him. She was scared, and she had a difficult time managing anxiety that resulted from fear. All too often, that anxiety turned into anger.

"Don't ignore me. I'm talking to you," the guy said, grabbing her arm and spinning her around. Gasps echoed up and down the lunch line, and everyone stepped back. People sitting at the tables nearest the confrontation stood up to get a better view. Edna couldn't take it anymore. She'd rather be in control of a tough situation than be in a chaotic one that was out of her control. She clenched her fist and drove it into the senior's groin as hard as she could. He doubled over and fell sideways to the tile floor. There was a collective groan of disbelief from the onlookers as the guy laid in the fetal position on the cafeteria floor, groaning.

Edna slipped out of line and sat down with Jenny. She was shaking. Her legs were bouncing under the table. "He just wouldn't leave me alone," she said under her breath. "He just wouldn't leave me alone..." She watched as teachers and lunchroom attendants huddled around the guy on the floor. Edna watched as students were questioned by the teachers. They just shrugged and walked away. She wondered if she'd get away with it when she noticed a teacher squatting down beside the senior. The guy looked up from where he was on the floor and pointed to Edna. The teacher nodded, stood up and walked over to Edna and Jenny.

"Did one of you punch that guy?" he asked.

"I did," Edna said, raising her hand.

"I'll be damned," he said, stepping back and sizing her up. "You took him down?"

"Yes sir," Edna said. She could feel her face turning red and could hear her heart pounding in her ears.

"Well, you need to come with me," he said.

"Okay," Edna said and walked to the office with the teacher. She sat down across from the secretary while the teacher went back and talked to the principal.

A few minutes later, the secretary's phone rang. "Yes. Certainly. I'll send her back now," the secretary said, and hung up. "Principal Horvath will see you now," she said. Edna got up and walked back to the office.

"Have a seat," Principal Horvath said and gestured to an open seat by the door. "And close the door behind you, please." She did as he asked. "Edna, how many times have I seen you in here this year?" he asked.

Edna shrugged. "Three or four times, maybe?" she said.

"Six, Edna. You've been in here six times this year, and each and every time was for fighting."

"I'm sorry sir," she said. "It's just that this guy was calling me a lesbian, and he said…" she looked down at her hands folded in her lap.

"Edna, I know that you've been through a lot, and I've cut you a lot of slack, hoping that you'd get it all out of your system. But now, I'm at a point now where I think cutting you slack is sending you the wrong message." He looked down at his clasped hands resting on the desk. "I'm going to suspend you for three days. I hope this will serve as a wake-up call. You *cannot* just punch and kick people when they upset you, no matter what they call you or say to you. You need to control your rage; don't let others control your rage. We live in a civilized society where that sort of behavior is just *not* acceptable. You get it, right?"

"I'm sorry," Edna said. "You've been very kind to me, Mr. Horvath. I don't know why I do it. It just happens. My mind goes blank, and I react."

"You're a good kid, Edna," he said. He sat back as if contemplating his next action. "I'm sorry we're here at all. I'm going to call your mom to come pick you up."

Edna went back and waited by the secretary for her mom. When her mom got there, she looked furious. "Edna!" she snapped.

"Sorry, mom," she said, looking down at her hands folded in her lap.

"Ms. Barrett, Mr. Horvath would like to talk to you before you take Edna home." She picked up the phone and dialed. "Ms. Barrett is here." Mr. Horvath came out of his office, smoothing out his shirt.

"Do you have any questions, Ms. Barrett?" he asked.

"No. You covered everything on the phone," she said.

"We'll have to have a meeting before she can return," he said. "You'll need to be there. Is there a time this week or on Monday that works for you?"

"It doesn't matter. Either way, I'm going to have to take time off work."

"How about Friday morning? Nine?" Mr. Horvath said, more to his secretary than to Edna's mom. The secretary nodded. "Nine? Does that work for you?" he asked Edna's mom.

"Yes. We'll see you at nine on Friday. Is this something that Edna should come to?"

"Absolutely. It's her future we'll be talking about."

A gift from God

It was a Saturday morning, and Joe was awoken by the early-morning sun peeking between his shade and window. He climbed out of bed and went downstairs, thinking that he'd get a bowl of granola cereal and watch cartoons like he did most Saturday mornings. When he got to the kitchen, he saw his mom getting ready to walk out the sliding glass door. "Where are you going?" he asked.

"Oh, good morning, Joe. You're up early. I'm going to weed the garden. You wanna to help?"

"I was going to watch cartoons," he said.

"Okay. I'll be out here if you need me," she said and stepped out onto the deck and shut the door behind her. Joe got his cereal and went down to the basement to watch the small TV; the only one in the house. After he finished eating, he grew bored and wondered what weeding involved, so he went back upstairs and opened the sliding glass door. His mom heard the door open and looked back at Joe from the garden. "Is everything all right?" she asked.

"Yeah," he said, standing in his Star Wars pajamas. "I just wanted to say hi."

"Go get your clothes on, and I'll show you the food we're growing," she said. Joe obeyed and returned fully dressed. His mom gave him a tour of the garden, showing him the corn, the peas, the lettuce, the strawberries, and finally, the rhubarb plant in the corner of the garden. The sun had not completely cleared the roof of their house, so the garden was divided into the light half and the shaded half. Joe was surprised at how much he enjoyed being in the garden. He inhaled the rich smell of the soft soil below him. He felt dew from the leaves christen his shins as he walked between the rows of the corn.

"Okay. Let's get to work," his mother said and lowered herself to a squat at the edge of the lettuce. She had a red bandana tied over her head and her long black hair flowed out the back.

"When you find a weed, grab it by its base and pull. Try to pull the roots out, otherwise, it'll grow back. It takes a gentle touch."

Joe squatted next to her and pulled a piece of crabgrass from the garden row. "Like this?" he asked, holding the weed above his head as if it were a trophy.

"Excellent," she said, taking the crabgrass from his nine-year-old hand and examining the dirty roots. She looked at him. "I had a dream about you the other night," she said as she turned her attention back to the row of lettuce.

"What about?" he asked as he lifted the plant leaves, looking for weeds underneath.

"In my dream, I saw you. Only you were a grown man," his mother said as she threw a pulled weed behind her.

"Really?" he asked.

"Yes, you were an important man. You were a diplomat and you spoke Russian."

"A diplomat? What's that?"

"That's someone who meets with kings and foreign leaders as a representative of the President of the United States," she said.

"Oh," he said, trying to grasp the meaning of everything, sensing its importance.

"Do you want to know something else, Joseph?" Her voice dropped to a whisper and she stopped weeding. "That dream came from God."

"From God?" he asked in awe.

"Yes, from God. He gave me a glimpse of how important you're going to be when you grow up. I think he did that, so I'd do my best to raise you."

"You really think I'm going to be important?" he asked, looking up at her touching a dirty finger to his chest. She nodded.

"After I had that dream, I prayed and I prayed, and after I prayed, I opened my Bible, and it fell open to Exodus. Exactly to the part where God was calling Moses to serve him and to free his people. That's not a chance opening of the Book of God. It's God telling me that my dream was real, and that it came from him. You, my son, are going to be a great man." She began weeding again. He tried hard to remember the word diplomat; he knew it was going to be important because he was going to be important.

Then fear crept into his heart. *I don't feel special. Maybe it's not supposed to be me. Maybe God made a mistake. Maybe Mother made a mistake. She'd be so sad, so disappointed, and it'd all be because of me. I'd be the reason she was sad,* he thought.

His heart hammered hard. It was more than his young frame could handle. His teeth clenched. Then he yawned, gasping for air. His heart seemed like it was pushing out of his body; every booming beat, pushing against his rib cage. He didn't know how to slow it down. He didn't know what to do.

And then there were little pinpoints of darkness that pierced through everything he saw, and those dark pinpoints grew and joined each other, blossoming together until everything was black. His eye muscles released their hold on his eyeballs, and they rolled back into his head, and there was relief. It was peaceful. He was gone.

He didn't know for how long, but he was gone. The next thing he knew, he was lying in the dirt, looking at the lettuce leaves hanging above him. He felt his mother on her knees next to him. She moved the leaves aside, and her face filled his world as she leaned over him. "Honey, are you all right?"

He saw fear in her eyes. She didn't dare touch him. He heard worry in her voice.

"I'm okay," he said.

"Surely, this is from God," she said. "What are the odds of me telling you what God told me, and then you passing out. This is certainly a sign. Thank you, God!" She smiled and looked at the sun rising above the roof line. They sat in the row for what felt like an eternity. She wept. "Thank you, God, for this gift."

Joe got up and wiped the moist dirt from his legs. His mother stared at him for a long time. She had to squint because the sun was so bright. "Wait right here," she said. She went inside and returned with a bowl and a knife.

"What's that for?" Joe asked. His imagination ran wild. He knew two things about his mom. One, she was deeply religious, and two, she was unpredictable. *Is she going to collect my blood in the bowl and have some sort of communion with it?* he wondered.

His mother saw his eyes grow wide. "Relax," she said. "Follow me." She took him to the rhubarb plant in the corner of the garden and cut a couple of stalks from the plant. They walked to the deck steps and sat down. "Put your tongue to this," she said, holding out the stalk of the plant. He did as she did.

"Ewww," he said. "It's so sour," he said. His mother laughed.

"Now dip it into this," she said and handed him the bowl. It was filled with sugar. She mashed the base of her stalk into the sugar bowl and then ate it. Joe did the same. "See, isn't that so much better? Isn't that a treat?" she asked. Joe nodded. They finished eating their stalks and sugar.

"Are you going to help me finish weeding?" she asked, putting the bowl aside.

"Would you mind if I went inside and watched cartoons?" he asked.

"Not at all," she said and turned her attention back to the garden. Joe watched as she dug her fingers into the earth and rooted out a piece of thistle and then moved on down the row, working from a graceful hunch. He went back inside to watch cartoons.

You wouldn't understand

The basement in Joe's house had been finished by the family who had lived there before them, and it seemed to be more of an afterthought than anything. The resulting family room was windowless and divided in half by a stairway, making it impossible to use the whole space all at once. A thick dark blue carpet ran through the entire basement, even under the washer, dryer, and utility sink, making spills and overflows soggy ordeals. All the furniture in the basement was on the opposite side of the utilities and staircase, which, along with the overabundance of carpet, only added to awkwardness and unplanned feeling of the basement.

Joe was sitting with his mother, listening to classical music, spinning from one of the records she had bought at a garage sale. She was sitting on the brown couch, folding clothes while Joe was on the floor, playing with Legos. The music floated through the large piece of fake-wood furniture that was the record player, and when the first song was over, applause burst from the brown cloth-covered speakers. Joe's mother began sobbing. He stopped building his spacecraft, walked over, and put his hand on her shoulder.

"Why are you crying?" he asked.

"I don't wanna talk about it," she said through her hands.

"Is it because it's so beautiful? The music?" he asked.

"No, honey, it's not because it's beautiful. You wouldn't understand." She looked up and tried to smile through her tears.

"You're just being brave now, aren't you?" he asked. His mother pulled him to her, hugged him, and rested her head on his shoulder, looking away from him.

"When I was a child," she said, "I used to walk from the parsonage, across the parking lot, to the church where my dad, your grandpa, used to work on his Sunday sermons. I played the organ while he was in his office. It was so much fun, playing loud music. I loved the fact that the notes came straight from *my* fingertips, and the music swirled around me and bounced off of the slanted ceilings and stained-glass windows, fluttering like a musical butterfly." She sat up and looked at him.

"Oh," Joe said. "Cool."

"One day, I was playing the organ, and when I finished the song, I heard someone clapping. I looked around, but the light from the stain-glass windows danced around the sanctuary like a kaleidoscope, confusing me in the dimness. Then the applause sounded from the blackness of the room, and it echoed throughout the shadowy sanctuary, but as hard as I looked, I couldn't see who was out there. And just when I thought I'd finally figured out where it was coming from, the clapping would stop and switch to another part of the church. It grew louder and louder, and I still couldn't locate the owner of the applause. I froze," she said, anxious air escaped from somewhere inside her torso as if she were there again. Joe had no idea what to do. He didn't want his mother to cry.

"It's all right," he said, patting her shoulder.

"And then, I heard my father's voice behind me, telling me how much he liked my playing. He scared me so bad that I jumped," she said, talking more now to herself than to Joe. "I asked my father how long he had been standing there, and he told me that he had heard the entire song. I thanked him for his clapping. He looked at me like I was crazy. He said that he hadn't clapped, and then I asked him who had been clapping then? He said that no one had been clapping. That scared me, Joe."

"I'm sorry, Mom. I don't really understand," he said and looked into her brown eyes for answers that weren't there.

"Joey, something bad happened that day," she said and returned to folding laundry as if the conversation had never happened. He stood there, not knowing what to do, desperately wanting to do the right thing, fearing that he hadn't. His mother continued folding.

"Well, what was it?" he asked, sitting back down by his Legos, looking to her for answers.

"I'll spare you all of the details, but I will tell you that I've never experienced rage like my father's rage. He questioned me. I told him about the invisible clapping moving around the sanctuary, and he thought it was the devil and demanded that all of the demons inside of me be gone in God's name. He struck me in the head numerous times to get the demons out." She folded a shirt and set it in the basket. “Sometimes, though, I can feel his rage surging through me when I get mad at you and Jessica. I don’t like it when that happens.” She looked up from her laundry to see if he was tracking with the conversation.

“I don’t like it, either,” he said. He looked at her and realized that he probably shouldn’t have said that.

“It doesn’t happen that often,” she said and continued folding the clothes.

“Yeah,” Joe said, appeasing her with compliance. “You’re right.”

“Please know that I love you terribly,” she said. “And know, too, that I’m not a perfect person and that sometimes I can’t control my temper,” she said. “It’s something that I’m working on.”

“Okay,” Joe said. “I love you, mom.”

“I love you, too,” she said and gathered her basket of folded laundry. She disappeared upstairs with the basket. He looked around the room, suddenly scared to be alone.

Death everyday

Jenny: Holy shit!!!

Edna: What?

Jenny: U R a hero

Edna: ?

Jenny: That senior you punched in the balls is a real asshole

Edna: Tell me about it.

Jenny: I guess he's an asshole to everyone

Edna: Ugh. Thinking about him makes my hand hurt.

Jenny: I guess he's a sexist homophobe

Edna: Not surprised! You wanna come over and hang?

Jenny: Can't The rents are out & I don't have a ride

Edna: Got it.

Edna: I got a strange email from Fisher today.

Jenny: English teacher Fisher?

Edna: Yeah.

Jenny: Does he wanna have sex with you?

Edna: NO!!!! Gross!!!!!

Jenny: Haha!!!

Jenny: What'd he say?

Edna: He asked if I was all right and he referred me to the social worker's office.

Julie: For the fight?

Edna: No. A poem I wrote for class.

Julie: ?

Edna: It was a dark poem. He said it was really good but it was also concerning.

Julie: Send it to me

Edna: The poem?

Jenny: Yeah

Edna: Okay. Wait a minute.

Edna: Here it is:

Death Everyday

Death sat atop her moist brain.
Its letters fused with her brain's gray matter,
seeping into the dark corners
of her thoughts, taking over
her life: school, friends,
family, conversations.
It was all she thought about.

I know… It's me…

I wish someone would bring a noose
over to my house
because I'd willingly
stick my head into it

and let that person
drag me like a dog on a leash
to a therapist's office
where they'd fix me.

Please drag your reluctant patient
into room number three.
We'll have her fixed
and ready to go by noon.

I know it's not that simple.
They can't just wash
the black rot of death
from my brain
and then return me
as good as new.

I know it's not that easy,
but I wish some relief were possible.
This pretending
like everything is okay
is killing me.

Jenny: Jesus Edna that's dark af

Edna: I know. 😊 That's why you love me. Right?

Jenny: Yes that's why I love you, but… Are u serious that's how u feel?

Edna: Of course not. I'm not serious.

Jenny: Phew!

Edna: Silly Jenny!

I'm sorry, Mom

Edna and her mother were ushered into the conference room next to Principal Horvath's office. There were no windows in the yellow meeting room. There was one big table in the center and mismatched chairs surrounding it. The florescent lights buzzed in their hanging metal housing, spreading artificial light around the room. Edna was surprised to see four people sitting around the large wood table. She recognized Principal Horvath, Mr. Fisher her English teacher, and the school social worker, but she didn't recognize the fourth person. She sat down next to her mother. *I wonder if Mr. Fisher will say anything about the poem?* she thought.

"My oh my, there are a lot of people here," Edna's mother said, looking around the room. "Are you sure you're all in the right place? A meeting for Edna Barrett?" she asked, half serious. Everyone politely laughed.

"Edna … Ms. Barrett, thank you for coming to this meeting today," Mr. Horvath said. "I want you both to know that I want nothing but the best for Edna." He looked at Ms. Barrett, and she nodded. "In the process of figuring out what's best for Edna, I've consulted with our team." He paused and gestured to Edna's English teacher and the social worker.

"Hello, Ms. Barrett. I'm Kathy Schumacher, the school social worker," she said and waved across the table. "It's nice to see you again."

"And as you both know, I'm Mr. Fisher, Edna's English teacher." He waved. He turned to Edna and said, "Hi, Edna. It's good to see you."

"Good to see you, too," Edna said and awkwardly waved.

"So, the tough news," Mr. Horvath said. "As you know, our team was in the process of evaluating Edna to get her the kind of help she needs. Now that process usually takes 60 days to complete, but since we opened the case study a little over a month ago, she's had two more aggressive incidents, and that's with everything we put in place at the last meeting to help her manage her behavior. So, despite the 60-day case study not being completed, we've decided that we're no longer able to meet Edna's needs here at Central High School." He paused to let it all sink in. He looked at Edna and her mother and continued. "We brought in an expert who knows how to deal with some of the things Edna's been going through."

"Ahh, what exactly does that mean?" Edna's mom asked.

"We think it'd be in Edna's best interest if we outplaced her to another school; one that would be better suited to meet her needs. At Steppingstone School, they're well equipped to help her work through her issues, teach her how to manage her behavior, and keep her safe. She's welcome to return when she's ready. Isn't that right Mr. Porter?" He gestured to the man who had been sitting silently at the end of the table.

"Absolutely. Hello. I'm Mr. Porter. I'm the intake specialist at Steppingstone School. We offer a small, supportive environment for students working through various issues," he said, leaning on the table as he spoke. "It's a wonderful, nurturing environment. Theoretically, Edna could be back here at CHS next semester if things go smoothly. We also have students who find that they enjoy Steppingstone so much that they choose to finish up their high school career with us. It's a good place to be." Edna's stomach twisted. She covered her belly with her hands, hoping that she wouldn't retch.

Edna leaned back in her chair, watching her mom's face turn red around her cheeks, and she saw the vein in her mom's neck bulge blue. *Not a good sign,* Edna thought. Edna's mom looked from face to face to face. She shut her eyes and took in a deep breath. When she opened her eyes, she said, "This is a lot to take in. I thought we were just going to talk about getting Edna back in school … The way you made it sound, Mr. Horvath, it was just a formality. I feel like you all just dumped this on us." Edna's mom strangled her pen. Edna couldn't remember the last time she had seen her mother that upset. "Forgive me, but I really want to swear at you all." She looked at the table and then back up at Mr. Horvath. "Especially you, Mr. Horvath." She dropped the pen onto the table in front of her, emphasizing her disgust.

"Ms. Barrett, I'm only looking out for Edna's best interests, here. I want her to work through her issues…"

"Her issues? What issues? You mean the loss of her father?"

"Ms. Barret, has Edna told you about the poem she wrote in Mr. Fisher's class?" Mr. Horvath asked.

"No," she said and looked at Edna. Edna shrank in her seat. "She hasn't said anything about a poem." Her words were sharp and short.

"Well, it played a minor role in us determining that we aren't really in a position to help her here," he said. "Mr. Fisher, would you care to speak to this?"

"Well, the poem was dark and made reference to depression and suicide," Mr. Fisher said. "I emailed Edna and brought it to the social worker's attention. Unfortunately, I didn't bring a copy of the poem to the meeting."

"Ms. Schumacher, would you care to speak to this?" Mr. Horvath asked.

"Sure," Ms. Schumacher said and shifted in her chair. "Ms. Barret, I'm sorry that I didn't contact you earlier, but I knew that we'd discuss it at the meeting today. After reading the poem, I didn't feel as if Edna was in any immediate danger, and I also think it's important to take into consideration that it was a creative-writing assignment. Having said that, though, I can report to you that it was a dark poem. Borderline concerning."

"Can I read the poem?" Edna's mom asked.

"Unfortunately, I don't have a copy of it with me, either," the social worker said. "I'm sorry. I can send you copy after the meeting."

"So, you've all decided to kick Edna out based on a poem that no one has a copy of?" Edna's mom asked.

"In all fairness, Ms. Barrett, Edna has been sent to my office six times this year for aggressive behavior. Those incidents are enough, in and of themselves, to call for an outside placement. That decision was made independently of the poem. So, I believe what everyone is saying is that the poem was simply confirmation that there is a lot going with her than we initially realized, and that an outplacement is what's best for her at this time."

"Okay, forget the poem, then. Mr. Horvath. Look at her. She's barely ninety pounds. She is *not* the aggressor, here. It's your school that has made her feel like she's gotta stick up for herself. What's happened to the others? The ones who instigated my daughter?"

"Ms. Barrett," Mr. Horvath interrupted, "no matter how you look at it, this school is not working for your daughter."

"Well," she said, collecting herself. "You might be right about that."

"What do you think, Edna?" Mr. Horvath asked.

"I don't know. It all seems like a lot, you know. I don't really want to do it," she said, sitting on her hands.

"We'll have to think about it," her mother said. "Can we do that? Can we at least have some time to process all of this?"

"Of course," Mr. Horvath said. "But I do feel the need to make one thing clear. Due to Edna's six incidents of aggression, she is not welcome back at school until she goes to a therapeutic school, and they give her clearance to come back. The Central school policy on aggression states that a student should be placed in an alternative therapeutic environment or expelled after the fourth aggressive incident in a school year. Now obviously, I've cut her a lot of slack here, but I can't do that anymore. I've already let two incidents slide. You don't have to go to Steppingstone, but that's our recommendation. If want to research other schools and you find one that better meets her needs, all you'd have to do is inform us, and we'd meet with that school. So, you do have choices, but honestly, they're limited right now. Steppingstone is the best one we've found in the area." He leaned back, gripping the arms of the chair.

"Ms. Barrett," Mr. Porter said. "I'm going to give you the paperwork for admission. It has been filled out. All we need is your signature."

"Can we have time to discuss this?" Edna's mom asked again.

"Absolutely," Mr. Porter said. "We'll hold the spot for Edna for three days, so I'd need this back by next Wednesday. Or if you want to just call us and let us know that you're coming, we'll hold the spot." He stood up and walked a packet of paper over to Edna's mom. "We'd love for her to tour the school. We could show her around as early as Monday morning. Would that work for you two?"

"We don't really have a choice, do we?" Edna's mom said, looking to Edna.

Edna shrugged and raised her eyebrows, looking around the table, wanting the meeting to be over.

"Well, that's it," Mr. Horvath said and stood up. He walked over to Mrs. Barrett. "I understand your anger. I'm sorry I wasn't clearer about the purpose of the meeting when we set it up. Please believe me when I say that this is very hard for me."

"Thank you, Mr. Horvath," Mrs. Barrett said, digging around in her purse, avoiding eye contact.

"I'll miss you, kid," he said and offered his hand to Edna.

"Goodbye, Mr. Horvath," Edna said and shook his hand.

"Get back here soon," he said. Edna nodded.

The car ride home was silent for the first few minutes.

"I'm so sorry, Mom," Edna said.

"I am, too," her mother said, staring straight ahead.

"I don't know what's wrong with me. I keep fucking up. I don't mean to mess up so much. I know it's the last thing you need," she said and leaned her head against the car window.

"Edna, honey," her mother said, softening her tone, "we all have a lot on our plate right now. Maybe this school will be good for you. Maybe they can help."

"I hope so," Edna said and drew a door in her breath that had collected on the car window.

When they got home, Edna went into her room and pulled the children's book *To the Moon and Back* from her bookshelf. She opened it to the page that housed the picture of her father she had taken on their ride home from their last walk through the woods. She tried to look past the thumb at her father's face. *Maybe he was fucked up, too,* she thought. *Maybe he couldn't control his temper, either. Maybe that's where I get it from.* She studied the picture for answers, finding nothing. Reluctantly, she put the picture back in the book and re-shelved it.

You'll be fine

Edna walked into the Steppingstone school office on Wednesday morning as had been discussed during the school tour earlier in the week. Her head swung this way and that; she was on high alert and had to find the source of every sound. Everything was foreign to her. New faces, none of them seemed friendly. New hallways. New everything. The school was housed in an old church building that smelled mildly of mold. The hallway carpeting had been matted down by decades of foot traffic, and the flooring underneath seemed to groan when stepped on. She looked at her mom as they sat down beside each other in the waiting area.

"You'll be fine," her mother whispered.

"I'm so worried, Mom. I don't know anyone here." Her mom took her hand and squeezed.

"You'll do fine. They'll help you out," she said and patted the top of her hand.

"You can both go in now," the receptionist said and gestured to the door of the principal's office. They both stood. Edna stretched and yawned an anxious yawn. She looked at the exit and fantasized about running out of the building. She followed her mother into the principal's office where she saw tall windows, floor to ceiling, along one wall that looked out to the courtyard where a stone statue of the Virgin Mary stood in the center. Edna could tell that the statue had, at one time, been a running fountain. There was a large vase next to the Virgin Mary where the water had been pumped; she could see the decolorization of the stone where the moss had grown when it was alive and flowing. Edna looked at Mary's face. *She does not look peaceful,* she thought. *She looks confused and worried.*

"Hi, Edna, we're so glad you decided to join our school," Ms. Deal, the school's assistant principal said as she whirled into the room. A young lady about Edna's age followed Ms. Deal in. She was smiling and seemed pleasant.

"I didn't have much of a choice," Edna muttered, and then remembering her manners said, "No offense."

"Well, you took the tour earlier this week, so you know the basic layout of the building. I'm going to have Kelly be your guide today. Her schedule is almost the same as yours, so she'll be able to help you out – get you where you need to go. This here is your schedule. The teachers' names and room numbers are listed to the right of the classes. It's all there. Kelly will help you today. Isn't that right, Kelly?" Ms. Deal asked.

"Yep," Kelly said. Just then the bell rang.

"Well, you two had better get to your first period class," Ms. Deal said and turned to Edna's mother. "Do you have any questions?"

"Not that I can think of right now," Edna's mother said. She turned to Edna. "I'll see you later this evening. I love you."

"I love you, too, Mom," Edna said and walked out with Kelly.

Edna and Kelly stepped into the bustling hallway. People were running from the entrance to their lockers to their classrooms. They all seemed to ignore each other. They were in their own worlds, looking at their phones before heading off to their classes. Teachers and staff lined the halls. They reminded Edna of the pictures she had seen of the stoic Queen's Guard. "There are a lot of adults in the halls," Edna said to Kelly.

"Yeah. Teachers and teacher's assistants."

"Assistants?"

"Assistants, staff, whatever you want to call them. They're here to help keep order. It's just one of the perks of going to a behavior-disorder school."

"Oh," Edna said feeling a little anxious, avoiding eye contact with the adults. She hated being stared at. She thought she could feel their eyeballs following her and Kelly as they walked to their class. It reminded her of the paintings in haunted houses where the eyes of the people in portrait paintings followed the spectators as they walked through the room.

"What'd you do to get here?" Kelly asked.

"Not much," Edna shrugged.

"Really? Not much?"

"I guess I got in some trouble at school."

"No shit, Sherlock," Kelly said. "Everybody here got in trouble at school. What'd you do?"

"I didn't really do anything," Edna said.

"You're going to play it that way, huh?" Kelly asked.

"Honestly, I really don't think it's any of your business," Edna said.

"Touchy, aren't we?" Kelly asked.

Edna kept walking.

"Let me guess ... You look like the type who goes for older men, maybe some daddy issues, right? You fell in love with your drama teacher, right? You gave him a hand job after school, and when he wouldn't blow his life up for you, you cut his dick off?"

"No! What are you talking about?" Edna asked.

"That's it, isn't it?" Kelly asked.

"You're wrong," Edna said.

The first class was math. Edna hated math. There were only five other students in the class, and the teacher seemed cool, but Edna had no idea what he was saying, or what they were learning. She looked around, wondering if she was alone. Of the five students, she seemed to be the only one paying attention. This worried her. She hoped that she would catch up quickly, and then she began really worrying: *What if I never catch up? What if I fall behind, and then I end up in a remedial class when I go back to Central? What if I never get into college because of this class?*

"Ready to go?" Kelly asked, snapping Edna out of her perseverating.

"Yeah," Edna said and followed Kelly to English class without saying a word. English was ordinarily Edna's favorite class, but this new teacher seemed stodgy; she had her gray hair tied up in a bun and wore a tweed skirt and matching jacket. Edna hated the poem they read. It was too dense and too hard to understand. She missed Mr. Fisher, her old English teacher. She had no hard feelings about his turning her poem over to the social worker. She understood. She was grateful that he cared.

Edna remembered what Mr. Fisher said that poetry should be more like punk rock ... more like Fugazi, than Bach. Poetry should be more like graffiti than fine art ... like Banksy, not Monet. He believed that if a reader couldn't tap into the central truth of the poem after the first read, then the poem was meant for academics, not the people. Edna missed Mr. Fisher and began to appreciate what she had had at Central. She made a mental note to send him an email, thanking him for everything he taught her. At that moment, she missed Central more than she imagined she ever could. *If only I would've controlled my rage,* she thought. *Then I wouldn't be in this hellhole.*

Then they went to art class, and again, Kelly said nothing to Edna in the hallway. It bothered Edna, but at the moment, she was more concerned about just getting through the day than she was worried about what was going on with Kelly.

"Hello. I'm Mrs. Stokely, and you can pretty much do what you want in here," the art teacher said. "There are supplies throughout the room – help yourself – go nuts. If there's anything you'd like to do, let me know, and I'll do what I can to help you out, or if you have any questions about technique or anything, I can help. Otherwise, you're on your own."

At first, Edna thought the whole setup was cool, but then she noticed that the other students were just sitting around the classroom, talking, and the teacher was on her computer the whole time. When Edna walked up to ask about a sketchpad, she noticed that Mrs. Stokely was shopping for cat toys online. Edna grabbed a sketchpad from the shelf and began doodling.

The bell rang, and everyone got up and headed to lunch. "You can eat with me," Kelly said. This surprised Edna. Judging by the cold shoulder that Kelly had given her all morning, she was a little worried about eating lunch with her. She assumed that she had somehow pissed Kelly off or something but wasn't sure how or what she'd done that pissed her off.

"Sure," Edna said. "Thanks." She hoped that lunch would give them an opportunity to get to know each other a little and get past any false impressions. Also, she didn't know a soul at the school, other than Kelly, and the thought of sitting alone in the middle of a lunchroom in a behavior-disorder school terrified her.

As she followed Kelly to the lunchroom in the basement of the old building, she could feel anxiety churning in her stomach and knotting her shoulders. When she got there, she froze on the edge of the cafeteria and soaked in her surroundings. There were small windows near the ceiling. The buzzing fluorescent lights lit up the gray tile floor and the matching cinderblock walls. Edna saw small pockets of friends laughing at tables together. Now, more than ever, she missed the relaxing lunch conversations she had had with Jenny safe at their everyday table in Central cafeteria. She very much doubted that Kelly could ever replace Jenny. Kelly made her feel uneasy; Jenny made her feel safe and calm and was always there for her.

That uneasy feeling was amplified as she looked around and saw staff standing around the perimeter of the lunchroom like prison guards. They occasionally redirected students to watch their mouth or to stop doing whatever they were doing. Edna was surprised at how responsive the students were. *For a bunch of kids at a behavior-disorder school, they sure are good at following directions,* she thought.

Edna got her food and sat down at Kelly's table. There were others sitting there. One guy looked high and was trying to grab food from his friend's tray. The whole cafeteria seemed to be filled with a *type* of student – a *type* with which she didn't normally associate. The overall vibe was one of anger and rebellion. *This isn't right,* she thought. *I don't belong here.* She desperately wanted to be back in the smelly cafeteria of Central High School, talking to Jenny about stupid shit.

"Everyone, this is Edna," Kelly said as Edna sat down. "Edna, this is everyone."

"Hi, everyone," Edna said.

"So, Edna, what brings you here?" a guy asked. He had long hair that hung like a curtain over one eye.

"I got kicked out of my old school," Edna said, dreading the follow-up questions.

"What for?" the guy asked.

Edna shrugged. "I don't know … Stuff," she said.

"I know why she got kicked out," Kelly said, smirking.

"Why's that?" the boy asked.

"She's blew her teacher and then cut off his dick," Kelly said and then made a gesture like she was cutting someone's dick off.

"No shit?" the guy asked, leaning into the conversation, his eye peeking from behind his hair.

"No. That's not true," Edna said, glaring at Kelly. "She's lying."

Kelly smiled at Edna. "I know you're type," she said.

"Oh yeah," Edna said. "What type is that?"

"You think you're too good for us. You think you don't belong here." Kelly's smile seemed sinister as she leaned forward, her elbows on the table, waiting for Edna's response.

"I don't think anything like that," Edna said, doubting herself, wondering if what Kelly said was true. She certainly didn't think she belonged there. "I don't think I'm better than anyone else," she said.

"Really? I think you're a stuck-up piece of shit who cut her drama teacher's dick off," Kelly said and smiled as she stood up and aggressively walked around the table toward Edna. Edna scrambled to her feet, stumbling backwards as she did. Kelly pushed her to the floor while she was stumbling backwards. From the floor, Edna looked at Kelly towering over her. Without thinking she scrambled to her feet and launched her fist upward into Kelly's chin. Kelly stumbled backwards. Just then two strong arms wrapped around Edna, squeezing the air out of her lungs, tipping her sideways and driving her shoulder to the floor. She struggled as a man laid sideways across her back, pinning one of her arms to her side with his thigh and the other with his forearm. She began kicking and then felt another person lay across her legs, pinning them to the ground. She looked up from the floor and saw Kelly face down in an almost identical position. It was the Steppingstone's staff, restraining both of them on the floor.

"You need to calm down," the man laying across her back said in a monotone, detached manner.

"I'm trying," Edna said. "You're not making it easy."

"As soon as you calm down and stop squirming, Roger, who is on your legs, will ease up. You'll slowly work your way out of this restraint," the man on top of her said.

"Okay. I'm calm," Edna said and rested her cheek against the cold tile floor, looking away from Kelly, staring at the various shoes and legs scattered around the room. She wanted to brush off the dirt particles that she could feel sticking to her cheek, digging into her skin. She could hear the guy restraining Kelly saying something similar about calming down and easing up.

"Okay, now I'm going to lift my weight off you. I'll still be here, and we'll go right back into the restraint if you get aggressive again, understand?" he asked, not waiting for a response. "After you've shown that you can be calm, we'll head back to the quiet room where we'll process what just went down. Do you understand?"

Edna nodded her head. She was embarrassed when she noticed a teacher urging the other students to get back to their meals. "Stop starring. It could easily have been you on the floor. I'd advise you to eat while you can because you're running out of time," the teacher said. "And we gotta go back to class, lunch or no lunch."

"Now Roger and I are going to be at your sides, and you'll stand up and follow us. If you follow us to the quiet room, we won't have to put our hands on you again. If you don't follow directions, we're gonna to have to escort you out of the room. You understand?" Edna nodded again. She was relieved that they weren't touching her anymore. She felt violated when the two men were lying across her body. She felt like she needed a shower to get the floor grime off her. It was like nothing she'd ever experienced before, a violation of being human. She thought someone should've explained that being thrown to the floor and restrained was even a possibility; it would have never happened at her other school.

The two men walked Edna past Kelly, who was still being restrained on the floor. She looked up at Edna. "Dick muncher," she said under her breath; a smile spread across her face as her chin rested on the tile floor.

In the small cinderblock quiet room with no windows, the man who had initiated the restraint had Edna sit on the floor with her back against the wall. He pulled up a chair and sat facing her. She looked him over with the interest of a victim who was trying to memorize her attacker. He was muscular and wore a polo shirt that said Steppingstone Alternative School in an arc on the right side of his chest. He wore khaki pants and low-cut, brown hiking shoes.

"So, Edna, I'm Scott. I'm a supervisor here at Steppingstone," he said, and waved. "As you obviously know now, we have zero tolerance for violence."

"Is that why you threw me to the ground? Because of your zero tolerance for violence? Because that felt pretty violent to me," she said.

"That was done for your own safety and the safety of the others around you," Scott said.

"Right," Edna said, crossing her arms over her chest, realizing that it might be a good idea to just stop talking.

"Suppose you tell me what happened?" he asked.

"I'd like to call my mom," Edna said.

"You'll see your mom at the end of the day."

"I'd like to call her now," Edna said.

"I'm not going to let you out of this quiet room until we process what just happened. That's school policy. When we're done, we'll call your mom together."

"I'd like to call my mom, now" Edna said.

"I've got all day," Scott said as he crossed his arms and leaned back in his chair. "I get paid by the hour."

"Fine," Edna said. "Kelly was starting rumors about me, and then she came over and pushed me."

"And?" Scott asked.

"And I hit her," Edna said.

"So, what could you do differently next time to make sure nothing like that happens again?"

"Not come back to this school," Edna said.

"What if that's not an option?" Scott asked. "And you have to come back. How would you make sure that doesn't happen again?"

"I wouldn't do anything differently," Edna said. "She was the one who started shit."

"I realize that there are things out of your control, but the way you respond to those things determines who you are and ultimately what happens to you."

"So, you're saying that I should have just sat there and let her beat me up?"

"No. Not exactly. There are staff around to make sure nothing like that happens," he said.

"You guys are the ones who hooked me up with Kelly in the first place. I didn't even know this type of stuff could happen."

"Well, I'm sorry you didn't know. It was in all the paperwork you and your parent or guardian signed, but that's beside the point. After an aggressive incident, we take the time to process the events, so you learn from them."

"Next time, I won't fight back ... now can I call my mom? I don't think I belong here," Edna said, covering her face with her hands. Edna's eyes tingled, and she feared that tears would fall, but they didn't. She was too exhausted and angry to cry.

"Okay," Scott said. "Follow me." He led her to the office and the phone. Edna picked it up, punched in her mom's number. Waves of anger swept over her as she waited for her mom to pick up the phone.

"Hello?" she heard her mom on the other end.

"Mom!"

"What's wrong? I almost didn't pick up because I didn't recognize the number, but then I wondered if it was you or the school."

"Mom. Get me the *fuck* out of here." Edna whispered into the phone.

"Edna. What's wrong?"

"I'll explain later. Right now, I need you to get in your car, drive over here, and get me out of this hellhole."

"Edna, dear, perhaps you're being a little overdramatic?"

"Mom. You know me. I'm never overdramatic. You need to get the fuck over here, now!"

"Okay. Is there anyone there who I can speak with?"

Edna looked around and saw Scott watching her from across the office. "No. Just get here now. A girl attacked me."

"What? Are you all right?"

"I'm okay. This guy, Scott, who works here threw me on the floor and laid on me."

"He laid on you?"

"Yes. Two guys laid on me," Edna said, staring directly at Scott when she said it.

Silence...

"Mom? Are you there?" Edna asked.

"I'm on my way," her mother said. Edna could hear the distress in her mother's voice.

When her mother got there, Edna sprang from her chair in the office and hugged her. "Are you all right?" her mom asked.

"This place is terrible," Edna said and buried her face in her mom's shoulder. She felt the release of anger and frustration as tears poured down her cheeks. She wiped them on her sleeve and stepped back from her mom. "Please don't make me come back here." Her mom dried a tear from Edna's cheek with her thumb and then marched across the office toward Ms. Deal's office door.

"Excuse me. Can I help you?" the secretary called after her.

"I'm going into speak to Ms. Deal," she said and went to the door and opened it. It slammed behind her. Loud murmurs worked their way past the door to Edna's ear. The meeting didn't last long. Her mother came out, walked across the room, and grabbed Edna's hand. "Come on. We're outta here."

How often does he visit God?

Joe's mother had gotten cards for his sister and him to fill out and give to their dad on Father's Day. This upset Joe because he wasn't able to pick the card out himself. He was also upset that he only had a card for his dad, nothing else. He decided to make something special for him, so he rummaged around his dad's workshop in the back of the garage and found a flat piece of scrap wood; he thought he could paint something nice on it for him, but it wasn't exactly square. There was a long, skinny piece of wood sticking up from the corner of the board. Joe thought he could get rid of it and make the board a perfect square. He went over to his dad's tool chest, which reminded him of a coffin, and pulled out a saw. He cut the piece off. He was proud of the fact that he was able to do it by himself. He then returned the saw to the enormous toolbox and took the wood to the basement where he painted a beautiful landscape scene complete with a blue sky, birds, a tree, and a large sun complete with rays. At the bottom of the painting, it said, "I love you Dad!"

It wasn't more than five minutes after Joe had finished painting that heard the garage door open, indicting his father's return from work. Then, he heard his dad yelling for him. "Joe! Joe!" he yelled.

"Yeah, what's up?" Joe asked as he came up the stairs. His father was holding the saw in his hand. "Do you know how this got bent?" he asked. "It was sticking out of my tool chest and the lid bent the blade." His father sounded upset.

"Well," Joe said, swallowing hard, "I used it to make a Father's Day gift for you."

"Great," his father said. "A saw for a Father's Day gift. It's ruined. Why were you using a saw without asking, anyway? You're too young to use a saw unsupervised." Joe was hurt by his dad's words, and his heartbeat rapidly. Blackness replaced his eyesight and his knees buckled. His last thought was, *I'd better brace myself,* and he put his arms out anticipating a fall to the cement floor.

Joe opened his eyes and saw his father and mother standing over him.

"He's coming back around," his mother said, gently patting his cheek. "See. I told you that it wasn't anything to worry about." She helped sit him up against the kitchen cabinets.

"You've seen this before?" his dad asked.

"Yes," she said. She looked at her son and said, "I think it's from God."

"What?" his father asked.

"I believe he visits God when he passes out."

"Is he all right?" his father asked, ignoring her. "You don't think we need to take him to the doctor or anything?"

"Do you want to take him?" she asked.

"I'd rather not pay for an ER visit if we can avoid it," he said.

"I'm okay," Joe said, waving at him. "I don't need to go to the hospital." He looked at the handle of the saw now resting on the tool chest and hoped that this incident would be that last he'd hear about the bent saw.

"How often do these episodes happen?" his dad asked.

"How often does he visit God?" his mother corrected him.

"Episodes," he insisted. "How often does he have these episodes?"

"Joe?" his mother asked, turning to him. "How often do you have these *episodes*?"

Joe shrugged. "I don't know," he said. "Once in a while."

"They need to stop right here and right now. This *God is speaking to him* stuff is ridiculous," Joe's dad said. "What if you're shopping, and he doesn't get a toy that he wants or something, and then he manipulates you with an episode, and then a clerk calls 911 or something? Then we'll be forced to take him to the ER or a specialist or something expensive like that."

"You don't believe these are real? That he's visiting God?" Joe's mom asked.

"What makes you think he's visiting God?" his dad asked.

"God told me that Joe is special, and that he's going to be a great man one day," his mom said.

"A great man?" his dad said and snorted. "God told you? Please."

"You're just jealous," his mom said. "You're jealous that God doesn't speak to you and that, one day, your son will be a greater man than you will ever be," she said. Joe could see her face turn an angry shade of pink.

"Jealous? Jealous!" Joe's dad said. "Why can't you just be happy with life? Why does everything have to be about God speaking to you? God showing you this or God showing you that?"

"You'll see," Joe's mom said. "Just you wait."

"Joe," his father said, turning to him. "No matter what your mom says, these episodes need to stop. They are not from God. Do you understand?"

"Yes sir," Joe said and nodded, and then he looked to his mother. He wanted to ask them how he should stop the episodes, but he thought it wasn't a good time to ask. *I'll try to not blackout,* Joe thought. "Can I have some water?" he asked, wanting to change the subject. "I'm really thirsty."

"Sure," his mother said and brushed by his father and went into the house to get Joe some water.

Why's the volume so low?

A gray cloud obscured the sun, and the sweltering summer day cooled. The morning rain drove Joe and Jessica inside. Their Mother handed them two thick brown towels as they stepped through the sliding-glass door. They wiggled out of their rain-soaked clothes and giggled at their nakedness and then put on warm, dryer-fresh clothes. They couldn't find anything but soap operas and news on the old TV that didn't have cable.

"We're *so* bored," they said, one echoing the other. After their mother's attempt to get them to read failed, she brought out an old, green milk crate full of records that she had picked up at a garage sale.

"Your job," she said, "is to look through all of these, listen to them, and tell me what's good and what's bad. Tell me what we should throw out."

Jessica and Joe eagerly started pulling out the records, looking at their covers. They put on record after record, listening to Tijuana Brass, Captain and Tennille, and Roger Whittaker. It was a wonderful way to fill the gray rainy day. They laughed. They danced and spun around each other. They lay on their bellies, their heads propped up by their hands, listening intently.

And then Joe pulled Johnny Cash's *Live at San Quinton* from the green, plastic crate. "Look at this," he said, showing the record to Jessica. They examined the backlit blue cover and tried to make out who exactly this Johnny Cash guy was from his silhouette. "This was recorded in a prison. Should we listen to it next?" Joe asked.

Jessica nodded, clapped her hands, and dropped them into her lap. She chewed her lower lip as she waited for the new sound. Joe worked the record onto the post and pulled the black lever down. They heard the mechanical dropping of the album and then listened as Johnny Cash began talking to the prisoners. Then he started swearing. Jessica sprang up and ran over to the record player to turn it off.

"No, don't shut it off," Joe said.

"We shouldn't be listening to this," she said over her shoulder. "Mom will kill us."

"Just turn it down," he said and scooted closer. Jessica turned it down. "There, that's good." He put his ear next to the speaker. Joe knew that his mom would be upset if she caught them listening to music with swears, and while he hated her erratic outbursts, he didn't think he'd get caught with the volume being so low. He smiled at Jessica as she sat down in front of the other speaker. They sat facing each other and listened to the whole first half of the record. They had just begun the second side when their mother popped her head into the room.

"What's going on in here?" she asked. "Why so quiet?"

"No reason," Joe said, a rush of adrenaline burst from his heart and surged through his body. He reached up over the edge of the record player and tried to stop it.

"We're listening to this," Jessica said and held up the album cover up for mother's inspection.

"That's nice. Why's the volume so low?" she asked, reaching over to turn the volume up for Joe and Jessica.

"Because there's swears on it," Jessica said looking at the floor. "I told Joe that we shouldn't be listening to it, but he said to just turn it down."

"You both know better than that," their mother said, her voice cracked with emotion. Joe knew he was in trouble and braced himself for the consequences. She reached inside the player and fumbled with the arm and needle. It made an otherworldly screech as it skidded across the black grooves. She yanked the record off the turntable with such force that it snapped in half in her hand. Her face turned red as she pinched both pieces of the broken record together and dropped them in the cardboard record sleeve.

"That's the devil's music," she said. Spittle flew from between her tightly drawn lips as she spoke. "Wait until your father hears about this. To your rooms."

She pointed to the stairs, and they both ran up them as fast as they could, not daring to look at each other. Joe was just happy to get past his mom and her temper.

When he was in his room, he paced around and around. He had escaped his mother's temper, but he knew he still had to face his father. Joe was uneasy. His mind traced the edges of the same thoughts over and over again. He kept thinking about his father coming home at lunchtime, and how angry he'd be. His pace increased. He looked out the window every time he heard a car pass, hoping it wasn't his father's.

On towards noon, he heard the low rumble of the garage door opening, and he knew his father was home. He put his ear against the bedroom door, trying to hear what his mother was telling his father, hoping that God had somehow worked a miracle and changed her heart, hoping that she wasn't as angry now that hours had passed. He heard her walking down the hall and ran to his bed and sat down. She knocked. "Your father's home. He'd like to see you in the kitchen." Her voice sounded sing-songy, as if she were somehow pleased.

He walked out and saw his father sitting solid on a chair at the dining room table. His belly filled his dress shirt and rolled out over his belt. His jacket and tie had been thrown over the chair next to him. Joe released a deep sigh, and the anxiety that had been building inside all afternoon escaped as his breath exited his body. Finally, it would be over, and he wouldn't have to worry about the consequences anymore.

"You know why you're here?" his father asked. His voice sounded tired.

"Yes. Because I was listening to the devil's music," Joe said.

"Come over here," he said. Joe walked toward him with resolve and leaned over his father's knee. Out of the corner of his eye, he saw his dad's large hand and raised high above his head, and then it came plunging down on Joe's backside.

Hard. The violence of the hit startled him. His father continued to hit him until Joe started to whimper.

"You know, this hurts me more than it hurts you," his father said. Joe seriously doubted that but nodded in agreement. He stood up, his hands covering his burning backside, and then his mother brought Jessica out.

"Hi, Daddy," she said.

"Jessica, do you know what your mother told me?" he said.

"That we listened to bad music," she said. Her demeanor changed as if she suddenly remembered she was in trouble.

"Yes. I'm afraid you're going to have to have a spanking for not turning it off when you should've."

"I'll take her spanking," Joe said stepping out in front of Jessica. His father looked at him and leaned back in his chair, not talking. He studied Joe.

"Why would you do that?" he finally asked.

"Because it's my fault," Joe said and turned to Jessica. "She wanted me to turn it off."

"Fine," his father said, and motioned for Joe to come closer. He bent over his knee and began the whole process again. His father swatted him, but this time, it didn't hurt. It was more of a tired ritual than a serious spanking.

"Okay, we're done here," his father said.

Joe's heart sped up, and anger pumped through his veins. *Why did he hit me so hard the first time and was almost gentle the second time?* Joe was surprised by how angry this made him, and the muscles holding his eyes in place let go, and they rolled back into his head. He tried to stop them, but he couldn't. He tried to massage them back down into place with his fingers over his eyelids, but that didn't work. Not matter how hard he tried to gain control of them and force them back down into place, he couldn't. He panicked. He feared that they'd stay rolled back inside his head forever. He also remembered what his father had said about not having any more episodes, and he panicked.

The next thing he knew, he was lying flat on his back on the brown carpet, looking at the underside of the dining room table. He father's strong hands wrapped around his ankles, and he dragged Joe out from under the table. His shirt rolled up under him and the thick carpet burned his bare back.

"Tom, you're hurting him!" Joe's mother yelled. "I told you you're way too rough with him," she said as she backed away. "What are you doing?" Joe could hear panic in her voice.

"He kicked me in the face," his father said as he touched his mouth with the back of his hand and held it up, bloodied, as proof. "He can't just kick me in the face and get away with it."

He then grabbed Joe by the front of his shirt and lifted him off the ground. They were eye level, and Joe's feet weren't touching the floor. His shirt seams dug into his armpits.

"Tom, please, it was an episode. He was having an episode. His eyes went back in his head. That was an episode," Joe's mother pleaded from down the hall. "He can't control his episodes."

"He's faking it. He knows full well what he did," he said and looked into Joe's eyes. His dull, gray eyes squinted. He stared at Joe as if he were trying to pierce his soul. He threw Joe away from him. Joe flailed backwards, desperately trying to catch his balance, scrambling to get his feet under his body. No matter how hard he tried, no matter how fast his feet moved, he couldn't right himself. The force of the throw was too great. He fell back and hit his head on the carpet. His father grunted and stepped over Joe as he walked down the hallway to his bedroom.

"Where are you going?" his mother asked.

"I'm going to take a nap," he said.

"Don't you want your lunch?"

"No," he said and shut the bedroom door behind him.

I'm not going back there

"Edna, get up. You can't just lay around forever. You've gotta do something," her mother said as she turned on the bedroom lights and pulled the comforter down from over Edna's head. Edna grabbed her covers and pulled them back over her head, determined not to let go of them.

"Leave me alone," she said. "I'm not going back to that school."

"I'm fine with that, but it's been three days now. I can't let you lay around here anymore. I called Mr. Horvath yesterday…"

"Can I go back?" Edna asked, lowering the comforter.

"No. He actually encouraged you to go back to Steppingstone…"

"I'm not going back there," she said.

"I told him that, and he said if you had to, you could enroll in an online high school, but that wasn't their recommendation, and they couldn't guarantee readmission to Central if you didn't follow their recommendations." Her mom sat down at the end of her bed and put her hand where Edna's foot was under the bedding.

"Let's do it," Edna said and sat up.

"I was looking online last night and narrowed it down to three schools that I thought would be good for you. I emailed you the links. You need pick one of the schools," she said. "I've gotta get to work now. We'll talk this evening."

"Okay. Thank you, Mom." Edna said.

"You don't have to thank me. I'm your mother, just doing my job."

"Thanks for putting up with me," Edna said and reached over and hugged her mom.

A parasite crawled inside of me

Edna opened her laptop to go through the schools that her mom had sent her. She froze when she saw the blue links. She was surprised at how much she didn't want to click on them. She didn't have the desire or the energy to read through the glut of information. She didn't know if she was lacking the energy, or she was just lazy, or she was just exhausted after what had happened at Steppingstone. She didn't really care, either. She knew she would disappoint her mother, so she hit the reply button to her mom's email and began writing.

Dear Mom,

I went to open the links you sent but couldn't bring myself to do it. I don't know what's wrong with me. I'm really worried. For the last few months, I've been feeling so sad, and I don't know where those feelings are coming from, and I'm sick of hiding those feelings. It's exhausting.

I'll try to explain. I don't want to disappoint you. At first it was like a fog had rolled into my life and dampened the colors to everything, which would be oaky if the fog actually stopped rolling in at some point. But it didn't. It kept rolling and rolling and rolling. I can't catch my breath. Now the fog is no longer just sadness. It's now smothering me. I only feel a little flicker of me at my core, maybe. Maybe not even that. I don't know what happened to the rest of me. I got engulfed in the fog. I'm lost. The colors are completely gone. Drown out by the fog. I can no longer see the things I used to love. What did I used to love anyway? Is love even real? Is the world pretending that there is something called love? Is it all a big joke? I no longer love. I don't feel anything but tired. Why is that? Why do I feel like everything has shut off inside of me? I don't feel normal.

It feels like a parasite crawled inside of me and started eating away at everything, including my soul. It's sucked everything out of me. I feel like an empty shell. Sometimes, I wish I had the energy to kill myself. Don't worry. I don't think I have the energy. I will tell you that I love you because I don't want to hurt your feelings, but I'm not sure that love even exists anymore. Sorry for the long rambling letter. I just thought I'd explain why I can't decide on a school today and where I'm at mentally and emotionally. This is all so pointless.

Love(?),
Edna

Edna clicked send and then typed "How do I kill myself?" into the search engine. The National Suicide Prevention Lifeline popped up in a large font – 1-800-273-8255. Edna ignored it and clicked past all the anti-suicide links. She clicked deep into the search-engine results until she found a suicide chatroom. She read about so many different ways to kill herself. Some of them seemed painful and scary, and some of them seemed too extreme. And then one stood out to her. *I can sit in a warm bath, take a shit-ton of sleeping pills, and wash them all down with a bottle of wine,* she thought. *I'd be comfortable, warm, and asleep, and I'd never wake up. I'd be relieved of this tortured consciousness.*

She got up from the computer and walked out to the kitchen, opened the refrigerator, and saw a bottle of unopened white wine cooling on the door self. *Okay, there's that,* she thought and walked into the bathroom. She opened the medicine cabinet and saw her mom's prescription sleeping pills staring back at her. She lifted the orange prescription bottle and shook it. *Okay. There's that,* she thought. She turned around and looked at the bathtub. She sat on the edge and turned on the water. She tinkered with the temperature until it was just right. She closed the drain and the tub began filling. She looked around for a clean towel and then laughed at herself. *What would I need a towel for?* she thought. Then she heard something downstairs.

"Edna! Edna!" her mom called and heard her mom bound up the stairs. She burst into the bathroom. Edna stood there. She frowned, and her face muscles felt as if they were set in concrete. Her mom looked at the filling bathtub. She leaned over and shut it off.

"I'm really scared," Edna said.

"I am too, honey," she said and pulled Edna close. "Can we go downstairs and talk about your email?" Edna's mom asked. Edna nodded. They walked downstairs and both sat on the couch, half facing each other.

"My life sucks, Mom," Edna said as she pulled her leg up under her on the couch.

"Your life isn't that bad, sweetheart..."

"My life isn't that bad? Are you kidding me?" she asked. "My dad died in a bizarre hunting accident, the kids at school hate me, I got kicked *out* of school, and then, at my new school, strange men threw me to the ground and laid all over me. Does that sound like things are going well? Just about every night, I dream about monsters and shadows pinning me down to the floor. I can't move. I can't get up. I can't escape. I melt into the tile floor and listen to the buzzing lights and the shadows laugh. And you know what's worse than that? I don't really give a shit about any of it. Fuck everything."

"Okay," her mother said, "I get it, but think about it like this, you have food and shelter, a safe place to live, me, and Jennifer, and please know that it's not going to be like this forever. Life gets better."

"I know," Edna said and began to cry. "None of it makes sense to me either. I'm exhausted even trying to explain any of it to you because I have no fucking clue why I'm so dead inside. I don't know how to even explain what I don't understand. It's so frustrating."

Her mother moved closer. She tucked an errant hair behind Edna's ear.

"I know I should be grateful, but it's hard. I can't shake these bad thoughts. Every time I try, they just come seeping back into my head."

"Edna. I had no idea," her mother said.

"Yeah. I just want to be done with everything. I feel like you'd be better off without me bogging you down ... maybe you could even get remarried without me around."

"Baby, that's terrible and so not true. I don't know what I'd do without you. You're my everything. I'm sorry you feel that way. How long have you felt like this?"

Edna shrugged. "I don't know. A long time."

"Please know that..."

"I'm scared," she said and leaned into her mom and cried.

"Okay. I get it," her mother said, stroking her hair.

"I've looked online for help, you know, looking for answers and support," Edna said.

"And?"

"And all I got were ideas."

"What do you mean ideas? Good ideas?"

"No. I came across this site where people were actually discussing, you know, ways to commit suicide, and I wanted to stop reading it, but I couldn't."

"Okay," her mother said. "What did you read?"

"Different ways that people did it."

"Did what? Killed themselves?" Edna's mom asked.

"Yeah."

"Sweetheart," her mother said.

"I read about taking a warm bath, drinking a bottle of wine, and taking sleeping pills..."

"Is that what I walked in on?" she asked.

Edna nodded. "I was thinking about it. I didn't know if I actually could do it."

"We should probably get you some help," Edna's mom said. "Are you okay with that?"

"I guess so," Edna said, feeling relieved and scared at the same time.

"Let me make some phone calls," her mother said. "Why don't you sit here in the living room and watch TV?"

"I just want to go back to bed."

"Honey ... please?"

"You don't trust me?"

"I'm scared. Please?"

"Okay," Edna said and pulled a blanket over her on the couch.

How important is that question?

"Mom, I'm not sure I belong here," Edna said as she and her mother followed a nurse through the emergency room, past rooms partitioned by sliding curtains, past moans and hushed conversations, past beeps and phones ringing, back to a little room.

"Okay, if you two will have a seat, someone will be here soon to ask you some questions and talk about what's going on." They both took a seat. The room was tucked back behind the ER and had a waiting room feel to it, but it was much smaller than the other rooms, and they were the only two in there. The carpet was an industrial brown, and the walls were a serene yellow with earthy prints hanging in frames that were screwed tight to the wall. There was a big, wide, wooden door that the nurse left open when she left. Edna got up and shut the door, so people wouldn't be able to gawk at her when they passed.

There was a soft knock on the door and a young man stuck his head into the room. "Hello. Can I come in?" he asked.

"Yes. Come in," Edna's mother said.

"Edna Berrett?" he asked as he entered, looking at the clipboard in his hand.

"Yes. I'm Edna," she said and raised her hand as if she were in school.

"Hi, Edna. I'm Scott," he said and shook Edna's hand. "And?" he asked, turning to Edna's mother.

"I'm Edna's mother," she said, shaking his hand.

"Her legal guardian?"

"Yes," she said, folding her hands on her lap.

"Okay, good. I work on the psychiatric unit here in the hospital," he said, looking over the chart. "It looks like you've been having some suicidal ideations?" he asked Edna. Edna looked at her mother for permission to speak about it. Her mother nodded.

"Yes. I've been thinking about it a lot," Edna said.

"Okay," he said, pulling the cap off a pen. "My job is to assess whether or not you're a danger to yourself or to others. I'm going to ask a lot of questions and then touch base with the psychiatrist on call, and she'll determine whether you should be admitted or not. If we do decide that you need to be admitted, we'll ask that you, or in this case, your mother, sign you in voluntarily. It saves a lot of paperwork, and you'll have more control of when you're able to leave. Any questions so far?"

"If you do admit her to the psychiatric unit, can I come along to see what it's like? To make sure she's safe?"

"Absolutely. You'll be able to visit, and if we do admit her, you're being there when she gets admitted will help the process go smoothly. So, yes, you'll be able to help check her in. I don't want to get ahead of ourselves, here, though. I have a few questions. First, are you currently on any medications?"

"No," Edna said, looking down at her hands.

"Have you ever been on any psychotropic medications?" Edna looked at her mother for help.

"No. She hasn't," her mother replied for her.

"Are you currently under the care of a psychiatrist, psychologist, or a therapist?"

"No," Edna said.

"Have you ever been admitted to a psychiatric unit or treatment facility?"

"No," Edna replied.

"Okay, moving onto psycho-social history. Have any immediate family members suffered from depression or anxiety?"

"No," Edna said. "Not that I know of."

"How important is that question?" Edna's mom asked.

"Depression is known to run in families. We only ask so we can get the clearest picture possible of what's happening with Edna," he said.

"Scott, can I talk to you in the hallway?" Edna's mom asked.

"Yeah. Sure," he said, and he followed Edna's mom as she ducked out of the room. Edna could her the edges of her mother's voice float around the corner, but she couldn't make out the details of what she was saying.

Edna's mom walked back into the room without Scott.

"What's going on?" Edna asked. "Where's the guy?"

"He'll be back in a minute."

“Okay,” Edna said, looking to her mom. Her mom looked away.

“Mom?” Edna asked.

“I need to tell you something.”

“What?”

“I need to tell you the truth about your father,” she said, studying her thumbnail.

“Dad? What?” Edna asked. Her stomach sank like she was on a rollercoaster.

“I didn’t tell you because I wanted to protect you … to protect his memory.”

“Mom? Tell me what?” Edna’s mind was racing.

“Your father’s death was a suicide,” she said. She sat down next to Edna, and put her hand on her knee, watching her reaction.

“Let me guess, a shotgun in the forest preserve?” Edna asked.

Edna’s mom took a deep breath and exhaled. “Yes. How’d you know?”

“People talk,” she said.

“Are you mad? Please don’t be mad. You were so young…”

“Were you planning on telling me? Ever?”

“Yes, but things like that never come up in everyday conversation, you know?” Edna sat and stared at the picture of a landscape secured to the wall across the room. “Talk to me, Edna. Please…" Her mom took her hands and held them.

"He was pretty messed up, wasn't he?"

"He was a beautiful person, Edna."

"I think I understand … I wish I could cry," she said, and tears began falling from her eyes. Her mom pulled her close and hugged her.

"Knock, knock," Scott said and stuck his head in. "Do you need another minute?" he asked.

"Yes. Please," Edna's mother said.

Shoot'em

He watched his father stack the borrowed guns wrapped in faded green padded sleeves into the trunk of his Caprice Classic. He climbed in and tried to fill the empty space between he and his father with questions. As his father drove, the white and brown winter landscape blurred past. Joe saw one cloud hanging all white and fluffy in the sharp blue sky, and he thought about killing jackrabbits. He wondered what it would feel like to kill something.

His father pulled off the paved road onto two ruts of earth, and they drove beside a barren pasture. He pulled over to talk to the farmer who owned the land. They laughed together; their warm guffaws visible in the icy air. The farmer waved and said, "Good luck," and they drove away.

Less than ten minutes later, Joe's dad pulled the car over, and they got out. His dad pulled a .22 rifle from its covered sleeve, loaded the magazine, and handed it to Joe. "This here's the safety," he said. "When you push it in, the gun won't fire. When it's out, and the red is showing, the safety is off, and the gun is live. Always walk with the safety on, and unless you're going to shoot, always point the barrel down to the ground. Got it?"

"Yes, sir," Joe said and took the gun from his father's rough hands, making sure the barrel was pointed toward the frozen earth. It was heavier than he thought it'd be. He loved its solidness and its significance. The smoothness of the wood and the cold black-blue steel barrel thrilled him. Power surged through his being. He couldn't believe his father had trusted him with such might, such responsibility. He followed his dad to the top of the hill.

"Shh," his father said, and stuck his arm out, preventing Joe from passing. "Look here," he whispered and blindly grabbed a handful of Joe's coat and pulled Joe to him, not once looking at him, just staring intently below. "Do you see that down there?"

Joe squinted. "Yes, sir," he said, his mouth dry with excitement.

"Take the safety off, line that jackrabbit up in your crosshairs, and then let 'em have it. Shoot'em," he said. Joe could smell the coffee on his father's breath, and the rising sun that bathed his face made his brown whiskers look orange. Joe did what his father told him. He exhaled, and a warm breath cloud spilled out around the cold, steel sighting mechanism. Joe squeezed the trigger. The gun spit out a sharp snap, and the sound bounced around the cold sky like a pinball.

"You missed," his father said flatly. "Next time, keep your eyes open."

They walked down toward where the rabbit had been.

"Look," his father said, pointing to the tracks in the snow. "You can see this, here, is where he was sitting, and here is where your bullet went. Pretty close." He sounded surprised.

Joe's feet grew numb as they spent the morning and afternoon walking around the barren fields, looking for jackrabbits that weren't to be found.

"We'd better get back," his father finally said.

As they walked toward the car, his father stopped short, like he had before.

"There's a cottontail," he said. "It's no jackrabbit, but it'll give you a good idea of what hunting feels like. How 'bout it? You wanna to take a shot?"

"Sure," Joe said, taking the safety off and lining the brown bunny up in his crosshairs. He held his breath, pulled the trigger, and the clean, sharp snap of the bullet exploding echoed off the trees into the cold air.

"I think you got 'em. There's another one," his father said, turning and pointing to another cottontail. Joe raised the gun and again squeezed the trigger. Through the scope, he watched the rabbit drop lifeless to the cold earth.

"That'a boy," his father said and tousled his hat. He briskly walked toward the rabbits. Joe had to run in fits and spurts to keep up. They found a splotched trail of blood leading into a batch of briars.

"Just leave that one," his father said. "It's not worth fishing out of those thorns."

His father walked over to the other rabbit and grabbed it by its hind foot. He held it close to Joe's face. Its limp body swung back and forth, echoing his father's oversized movements. Joe had shot it above the eye. Its skull caved in, collapsing a quarter of its cranium.

Joe imagined the bullet crashing into the rabbit's skull, and his eyes rolled back into his head, and they locked into a comfortable position offering only black, no sight. Joe blacked out, and in the blackness, he had a vision of lying underneath the briar patch in the noonday sun. A screeching sound pierced his ears. He couldn't catch his breath. He tried but couldn't get enough oxygen to satisfy his panicked brain. A sharp pain boomed through the side of his head, just above his eye. He reached up and found a hole where the pain was stemming from. He felt crushed skull bone beneath his fingertips; he could move them around like loose puzzle pieces. He heard flies buzzing around the hole; their tiny fly feet skitter across his forehead. He tried to swat them away but couldn't move his arms. He panicked and tried to get free. His entire body wouldn't respond. Warmth spread across his midsection as his bladder empty. He knew that he'd wet his pants.

And then little pinpoints of sight pierced through the darkness, and those little pinpoints expanded into his father's silhouette, outlined by the sun, standing over him.

"You back?" he asked.

"Yeah," Joe said, sitting up, shaking the snow off his hands. He saw the dead rabbit lying beside him.

"You wet yourself," his father said.

Joe scrambled to his feet, trying to manage his footing as he rose from the ground. He stood in the middle of the bright, afternoon sun, under the gray cloudless sky. He surveyed the area that he had rolled around in during his blackout. In some spots he had scuffed down, working through the snow to the Earth's dirt. It looked as if he had even rolled over the dead rabbit crushing its carcass flat.

He wondered what his father had been doing while he was rolling around on the ground. *Was he just standing there, watching me? Did he try to help?*

A hatchet hacking away

The bright morning sunshine angled through the kitchen window above the sink. Edna stopped when she heard the birds chirping through the closed window. She opened it a little to hear them more clearly. Her mother walked in wearing her tattered old bathrobe and dragging her well-worn slippers across the tile floor.

"It's a beautiful morning, isn't it?" her mother asked.

"It is," Edna said as she reached for her semi-translucent prescription bottle of Zoloft, sitting in the middle of the table. She knew her mother insisted on keeping it there so she wouldn't forget to take them. It was a nudge, a gentle reminder; it showed how much her mom cared. Edna smiled.

"Do you think the medication is helping?" her mother asked.

"It's amazing," Edna said. "I don't remember feeling this good. It makes me feel sleepy sometimes, but in general, it's really helping," she said as she popped one into her mouth and washed it down orange juice.

"That reminds me of what your father used to say," her mother said.

"About meds?" Edna asked.

"Yeah. He used to compare his depression to a vine that slowly strangled the life out of a tree. He was the tree, obviously. He always said that his antidepressants were like a hatchet hacking away at the vines that strangled the life out of him."

"Yeah, I can see that," Edna said. She stopped eating her cereal and stared at the wall across the room.

"Are you okay, honey? Did I upset you?"

"No. Not at all. I was just thinking that I really wish he was here, you know, so we could talk about it."

"About depression?"

"Yeah…" Edna said and continued eating.

"Will you promise me something?" her mother asked.

"What?"

"That you'll never do anything, like commit suicide, without letting me know where you're at, you know, mentally, so I can get you some help?"

"I can do that," Edna said.

"It's a promise then?" her mom asked holding up her little finger.

"Pinky promise," Edna said, locking their fingers together.

U r so proper

Edna loved online school. She loved the control she had; she could flip the computer open and attend, and then when she got tired or frustrated, she could shut the laptop and take a nap. She liked that she was able to pick the specific classes she wanted to take to meet her requirements, and that she was able to work at any time she wanted, not just between the hours of 7:30 and 3:00. She was also surprised by the social aspect of the online school. While the teachers were not always online, there was usually someone enrolled in the class who would get in touch with her within an hour or so if she posted a question in the class's chatroom. That's how she met Shane.

Edna: Re the paper on the poem assigned this week -- Does anyone know if we need to identify all of the figurative language we've discussed so far or if we just need to focus on similes and metaphors? PM me if you want. Thanks!

Shane: hey! just similes and metaphors that's all im doing i looked at the rubric n that's all she's grading us on

Edna: Thanks Shane!

Shane: ur up late

Edna: Yeah can't sleep. You?

Shane: me either

Edna: Where are you?

Shane: near chicago u?

Edna: I'm in Norwood. A small town in MN. Do you like Chicago? I've never been.

Shane: i <3 it so cool   it'll be cooler when m older

Edna: How old are you?

Shane: 19   Chicago will be cool when m 21 bars everywhere how old r u?

Edna: I'm 17. I'll be 18 next month.

Shane: uh-oh

Edna: Uh-oh what? Why?

Shane: jail bait…

Edna: Gross…

Shane: j/k lol

Edna: I've always wanted to visit Chicago. I want to leave this little town. Seriously it's so small there are no stoplights. There are 3 bars and 4 churches. There are 103 people in my grade. Well there were 103 people in my grade.

Shane: Why r u in online school?

Edna: Ehh…

Shane: u'd rather not say?

Edna: Yeah. You?

Shane: that's bold

Edna: What?

Shane: u'll ask question u won't answer

Edna: Sorry.

Shane: j/k lol i got k/o for selling drugs

Edna: I got kicked out for fighting. They sent me to an alternative school.

Shane: me 2! I got k/o'd of the alternative school went to rehab m trying to get my shit 2gether 2 get in 2 college

Edna: I got in a fight on my first day there. I wouldn't go back. I want to spend my senior year in my old school. I miss it.

Shane: send pic?

Edna: I don't even know you.

Shane: m not trying 2 b creeper m not asking for a boob shot just want to know who m talking 2

Edna: You send me one first.

Shane: K

Edna: Okay.

Shane: u r so proper

Edna: What do you mean?

Shane: messaging u is lik emailing my granny w/ periods n shit

Edna: Sorry. Maybe it's my OCD (haha!). I need to use punctuation, or I can't hit send.

Shane: Rly?

Edna: I don't have OCD, but I do like using proper grammar.

Shane: email address 4 pic?

Edna: Yes. Here: ednabarrett1234@gmail.com.

Shane: Kewl chk 4 a pic

Edna: Cool. Later.

Shane: L8er

Id like 2 meet u 2

Shane: u up?

Edna: Hey how are you?

Shane: k been better u?

Edna: I'm doing all right I guess. Bored af. Working on homework.

Shane: af ha! I lk it!

Edna: 😊

Shane: went 2 court 2day bad news

Edna: Oh no. What happened?

Shane: pressed charges m going 2 have 2 serve 40 hours of community service and stay out of trouble 4 a year if trouble in year m going 2 get locked up w/ big boys

Edna: You've been to juvie before? Locked up?

Shane: 1 time

Edna: What'd you do? How long?

Shane: 2 mos long story u get it rght?

Edna: Maybe? Lots of questions though.

Shane: hey! ur bdayz soon right?

Edna: Two weeks!

Shane: hbd!

Edna: You're a little early.

Shane: got n idea!

Edna: What?

Shane: y don't I drve up 2 see you in mn? what waz town again?

Edna: Haha! I live in Norwood.

Shane: punched town in2 phone could be there in 7 hrs

Edna: Stop. Just remember to wish me a happy birthday two weeks from today. That's all…

Shane: soundz like u don't want me 2 come up?

Edna: It's not that I don't want you to come up. I'd like to meet you sometime, but…

Shane: boyfriend?

Edna: No. I told you that I don't have a boyfriend. I just don't know how it would work out. I live at home with my mom and she's not going to let you stay here. I can just imagine explaining that I met a boy online and he's coming to visit me. She'd freak out!

Shane: sounds like a tightwad what if she never knew? what if i styed @ hotel? id come 2 see u whenever I could she wld nvr know

Edna: Tempting. Let me think about it. I really would like to meet you & she's not a tightwad she's just looking out for me.

Shane: i get it lmk id like 2 meet u 2

We're just friends

Edna: How are you?

Jenny: Ok

Jenny: Miss seeing u everyday

Edna: Yeah. Me too. I get to see you on Sunday, right?

Jenny: Yup!!! Birthday girl!!!

Edna: I can't wait.

Jenny: School sux without you

Edna: I know. It sucks not seeing you every day.

Jenny: I know u don't want to hear it but since u left Ive had to totally scramble to find a new squad to hang with

Jenny: I needed someone to eat lunch with

Jenny: It's lonely w/o you

Edna: Ugh. You're breaking my heart. I'm sorry! Who are you hanging out with?

Jenny: Jody and her squad

Edna: How's that going?

Jenny: It's fine

Edna: Fine?

Jenny: Fine if u don't mind talking about makeup and clothes all the time

Edna: Sorry. I know those aren't your favorite topics. I hope I'll be back soon.

Jenny: K

Edna: Guess what?

Jenny: What?

Edna: I met a guy.

Jenny: WHAT???? Spill the tea!!! 😊!!

Edna: I told you about this online school, right?

Jenny: U met him online?

Edna: Yes! His name is Shane.

Jenny: And?

Edna: He's nice and funny. We've Facetimed. A lot. He's cute. I'm obsessed with his voice.

Jenny: Where's he from?

Jenny: Any chance for me to meet this new bf?

Jenny: Pic?

Edna: Here... Isn't he gorgeous? BTW - we're not exactly bf and gf. We're just friends.

Jenny: Whatever!!!...He's hot af!!!

Edna: I wouldn't mind being his gf though...

Edna: Never mind. It'll never happen. How are you?

Jenny: I'm good

Jenny: Same boring shit Mom's being a pain in the ass like always We'll talk more on Sunday

Jenny: You can tell me more about Shane

Edna: See you Sunday!

Jenny: Sunday, Sunday, Sunday!!! ((Echo effect))

Edna: 😊

Maybe we won't park at the top today

On her birthday, Edna woke up a little early and rushed through her online homework. She half expected to see Shane online, doing his homework, too, but then she realized that it was too early for him to be online. She wanted to get everything done early, so nothing was hanging over head when her mom took her to the Mall of America for lunch at Tucci Benucch. Edna loved the baked spaghetti, and then, after lunch, her mom was going to take her shopping for some new clothes. It was a tradition. In general, she hated drawing unnecessary attention to herself, and her birthday was no exception; however, this annual trip to the Mall of America was one of the few things she looked forward to every year.

On the hour-long car ride, Edna played her favorite playlist for her mom and explained why she liked each song, giving her the dirt on what she knew of each of the musician's personal life along the way.

"So, mom, don't be mad, but I met a guy," Edna said.

"What?" she said. "Where?"

"Are you mad?" she asked before she continued.

"Not at all. That's totally age appropriate. Unless..." She raised her eyebrows and looked sideways at Edna.

"No. No. It's nothing bad. I met him online. We just talk a lot. I really like him, but we're just friends."

"You understand, right? I have to ask…"

"What?"

"You haven't sent him any dirty pictures or anything like that, have you? Because that stuff stays on the internet forever. Please tell me you haven't."

"Oh my god, Mom. Are you being serious right now?"

"I just worry about you," she said.

"No. I wouldn't do that," Edna said, turning to look out the window. "Ever."

"So…?"

"So what?" Edna asked.

"So, tell me more,"

"Well, he lives just outside of Chicago, and he makes me laugh. I'm so comfortable around him…"

"Around him? You've met him?"

"No. Not in person. We just hangout on the phone. We facetime and talk that way."

"Oh."

"Oh, what?"

"I just didn't realize that that was going on. How much time do you spend taking to him?"

"Mom! I just want to tell you about him and let you know what's going on in my life. I'm okay. You don't need to freak out."

"I'm not freaking out. I'm just concerned. You'll understand when you have kids." Edna rolled her eyes. "Go on. I'll listen. I won't interrupt any more. I want to know about him."

"He's so sweet. He always asks how I'm doing, and he sends me random texts throughout the day, just asking what I've been up to and telling me that he's thinking about me."

"He sounds like a nice boy."

"He is. I really like him."

"Can I meet him?"

"You mean like, Facetime him?"

"Yeah. Maybe you can introduce me the next time you talk to him," she said and looked to Edna. "It wouldn't have to be a big deal. I'd just say 'Hi' and move on."

"Yeah, sure. I guess that'd be okay. You have to promise not to embarrass me, though."

"I promise you that I'll *try* not to embarrass you," her mom said as they pulled into the parking garage and drove toward the top.

"Why do you always drive up to the very top?" Edna asked.

"Because I know no one else drives to the very top unless the lot is full, and I know I'm guaranteed parking up there. I don't mind riding the elevator, either. That's why."

"Did you know that these Mall of America parking garages are a hot spot for suicides?"

"What are you talking about?" her mother asked, almost stopping the car. Looking at her sideways.

"These parking garages are so tall, and nobody is watching them, so kids come up here to kill themselves."

"How do you know this?"

"How do you not? I thought everyone knew that."

"That's terrible."

"It's just a fact," Edna said, looking out the passenger window.

"Edna…" her mother began.

"No, Mom, I'm not suicidal," she said.

"You'd tell me…"

"Yes, Mother. I'd tell you."

"Okay," she said. "Maybe we won't park at the top today," she said, pulling off onto the fourth level of the parking garage.

What are you doing here?

Edna sat the shopping bags on the seat next to her and inhaled in the smell of mall-store newness: new shoes, a new watch, and new clothes. She was just the right amount of full, too; discomfort hadn't quite set in. Had she indulged in one more bite of food, she might feel a little differently. She fastened her seatbelt, leaned her seat back, and let the movement of the car and the buzzing of its tires lull her to sleep. Falling asleep on the way home had become as much of a tradition as the birthday trip itself.

"Edna. Edna, dear," she heard her mother say. "Honey wake up. Are you expecting someone?"

Edna sat up and rubbed her eyes. She saw a car sitting in their driveway and a man's silhouette on the driver's side. "No. Jenny's coming over, but not until I text her."

"I wonder who that is?"

"Oh no!" Edna said, sitting up straight in her seat.

"What? What's wrong, Edna? You're scaring me."

"I wonder if it's Shane?"

"Shane? The boy you talk to online?"

"Yes. Look at the license plates. They're from Illinois." Edna's mom pulled into the driveway behind an old car, a white Chevy Caprice Classic.

"Do you think he's okay? He didn't move when we pulled in. Do you think he's dead?" Edna's mother asked.

Edna unbuckled her seatbelt and grabbed the door handle. "Whoa, just where do you think you're going?"

"I'm going to say hi."

"We don't even know who that is," her mom said, grabbing her arm. "Maybe we should call the police."

"Don't be ridiculous," Edna said, looking at her mom, waiting for her to let go of her arm.

"Well, I'm going with you. You can never be too cautious," she said as she reached into her purse and pulled out a can of pepper spray.

"Mom!" Edna said. "Pepper spray?" Edna knew that her mother had carried pepper spray in her purse since she went to nurses' aid school, decades ago, in Minneapolis, but she'd never seen her pull it out.

"I told you this would come in handy someday," she whispered.

Edna's mother walked in front of her, protecting her as they approached the car. Her fingers strangled the small pepper-spray canister. Edna struggled to look over her mom's shoulders, bobbing from side to side, trying to catch a glimpse of whoever was in the car. They made their way to the driver's side window; it looked as if the passenger had fallen asleep. Edna's mom knocked. The passenger jumped in his seat, startled. Edna's mom reflexively squeezed the pepper-spray trigger. The spray hit the closed window and splattered everywhere.

The smell was overpowering. Edna and her mother doubled over and gaged as wafts of spray hit the back of their throats, and while neither had been directly hit, their eyes began to water as the spray lingered in the air and burned their senses. Edna began rubbing her face, which only made the burning worse. Her nose began to run. Through her tears and snot, she saw Shane sitting in the car on the other side of the window. He looked horrified; his hands were raised up in the air as if he were being held up.

"Shane! What are you doing here?" Edna asked, wheezing as she spoke.

"I'm here for your birthday," he said, his words muffled by the car window. He looked to Edna's mom.

"That's my mom," Edna said as she put her hand over her mouth and coughed.

Edna's mom waved, "Hi," she coughed. Shane waved.

"Are you going to get out, or are you just going to sit there?" Edna asked.

"Yeah. Yeah," he said, hurriedly, and popped the door open.

"Let's go inside and get cleaned up," Edna's mom said.

"Come on Shane," Edna said and gestured for him to follow her. "You can get something to eat and watch TV while we shower this crap off of us."

Edna found herself in a conundrum after she had showered; should she take time to do her hair and get fancied up, or should she skip the primping and hurry back to Shane? As she contemplated this, she heard the tinklings of conversation between Shane and her mom float down the hallway. She worried that her mom would say something stupid or ask him a bunch of questions that would scare him off. And then she remembered why Shane had been kicked out of school. *Drugs!* She knew if he mentioned that he'd sold drugs, any chance of him becoming her boyfriend would be stopped right there in their tracks. Her mom may even kick him out of the house, tactfully of course, but she'd, no doubt, make her feelings known. Edna brushed her hair as she hurried down hall.

"What are you two talking about?" She asked as she walked into the living room, pulling the brush through her tangled hair.

"Oh. Nothing, really. Just learning a little bit about Shawn," Edna's mother said.

"Shane. His name is Shane," Edna said.

"Oh. Shane. Sorry. I've been calling you Shawn for ten minutes now, and you didn't say anything. Why wouldn't you correct me?"

Shane shrugged and took a sip of root beer.

"Mom leave him alone. He's probably scared of you after you tried to take him out him with pepper spray."

"I didn't spray him with pepper spray."

"You tried," Edna said.

"Shane, I'm assuming you'll be joining us for dinner and some cake?" she asked.

"Of course, he'll be joining us for my birthday evening," Edna said. "I'll text Jenny now and let her know what time to be over for pizza, cake, and a movie. Sound good, Shane?"

"Yeah, that sounds great," Shane said.

"Shane..." Edna's mother said.

"Yeah," he said.

"You're from Chicago, right?"

"Yeah," he said. "Actually, a suburb just outside of Chicago."

"And I'm assuming that you aren't planning on driving back there this evening, is that correct?"

"Yeah. It's a long drive," he said, fiddling anxiously with the top of the soda can.

"Do you have friends or family in the area?" she asked.

"No, ma'am."

"What exactly are your plans for tonight?"

"Well, I guess I hadn't thought past getting here and surprising Edna for her birthday ... I guess I could stay in a hotel," he pulled out his wallet and thumbed through the money inside, "but I've only got enough money for gas on the way home."

"Edna, honey, maybe you and I should have a private sidebar, here," Edna's mom said and walked toward the kitchen. Edna followed.

"Mom. Can't he just stay here?" Edna asked, leaning against the counter. "He drove all this way."

"Edna. Really. I don't know this young man from Adam. He could be a serial killer, for all I know."

"Mom. Trust me, he's not a serial killer. He's a good guy."

"Edna, please look at this from my point of view. You tell me, today, that you met a guy online, and then he drives hundreds of miles and just shows up at our house. And you've never met the boy in person, and now you want me to open my house up to him? No way! What if he rapes you while you're sleeping?"

"Mother! Please! Keep your voice down. He's not going to rape me. We've talked for hours online..."

"I'm sorry. I'm putting my foot down. He can stay for pizza, cake, and a movie, but then he has to go."

"Go where? Back to Chicago?"

"No. I'll get him a room at the Prairie House. I'll call now and pay over the phone. All he'll have to do is check in at the desk. He can stop back here in the morning for breakfast before he heads home if he wants." She picked up her phone and called.

Edna walked back into the living room and plopped down on the couch next to Shane. "So, she's going to get you a room in a hotel the next town over. Is that okay?"

"Yeah," Shane said. "I get it. She doesn't know me."

"You can stay here this evening for pizza, cake and the movie, but then you'll have to head over there." She waited for his reaction. "She said you could stop by in the morning for breakfast."

"Fine by me," Shane said.

I'm clueless about Clueless

The kitchen was filled with the smell of pizza: fresh baked crust and melted cheese. Edna loved the pies from Unhinged Pizza. On her birthday, she always had her mom order more pizza than they'd ever be able to eat in one evening because she loved the leftovers; she ate them for breakfast, lunch, and dinner until it was gone. She was grateful that there was enough pizza for everyone now. Her chocolate cake with vanilla frosting, that her mom so lovingly made for her every year, was sitting on the counter with the candle numbers 18 planted into its uneven frosted surface.

"Is everybody ready?" Edna's mom asked as she turned off the lights and lit the candles. "A one, a two, a three. Happy Birthday to you…" They all sang and laughed at how out of tune it sounded. Edna smiled at Shane. Shane smiled at Edna. She blew out her candles.

"Did you make a wish?" Jenny asked.

"Oh yeah," Edna said and smiled at Shane.

"What'd you wish for?" Shane asked.

"I can't tell you, or it won't come true."

"Come on. What'd you wish for?" he insisted.

"Shane," Edna's mom said, "you don't want to ruin the wish, do you?"

"No. I was just curious," he said and blushed.

"Okay, Shane, here's how it works," Edna said, handing him a large plate. "You load up on pizza and cake, so you don't have to come back in during the movie. We only pause for emergencies."

"Cool," Shane said. He loaded his plate with pizza and cake. "What movie are we watchin?"

Jenny giggled and looked at Edna and Edna's mom. "You're so going to hate this movie," she said and laughed.

"Shane, I'm afraid you've stumbled into a little tradition that may come across as a little girly to you," Edna's mother said.

"Okay," he said, nodding his head. "I'm the one crashing the party. I get it."

"The movie is Clueless," Edna said. "Are you familiar with Clueless?"

"Nope," he said, fumbling for a napkin. "I guess you could say I'm clueless about Clueless." He laughed. Jenny looked at Edna and rolled her eyes.

"Clueless was one of my favorite movies when I was a teenager," Edna's mom said. "It's a modern-retelling of Jane Austen's novel, *Emma.*"

"I have no idea what any of that means," Shane said, "but, like I said, I'm the guy who crashed your party. I'm just happy to finally meet and hang out with Edna."

"It's a cult classic. We watch it for my birthday every year," Edna said.

"Cool," Shane said.

Everyone filed into the living room. Edna's mom sat down in her chair, leaving the couch to everyone else. Jenny and Shane stood there, staring at the couch as if they were waiting for a crossing guard to tell them that it was safe to cross the street. They weren't sure how to seat themselves.

"I'll sit in the middle," Edna said as she lowered herself onto the couch careful not to spill her plate full of food. Shane sat on one side of her, and Jenny sat on the other. Shane took up more space than Edna had anticipated he would. He his legs were wide apart. Edna had to sit at an angle to accommodate his man spread. Edna's legs now jutted into Jenny's personal space. Jenny was wedged tight into the corner of the couch. She looked at Edna and raised her eyebrows. Edna shrugged and gave an expression that said, *What do you want me to do about it?*

"You know what?" Jenny said, scooting off the couch to the floor. "I'll sit down here and eat."

"Thanks, Jenny," Edna said. Her face communicated more appreciation than her words conveyed.

"No problem," Jenny said. "I get it."

"Is everyone ready?" Edna's mom asked as they all settled in for the movie. "Here we go!" She hit play.

Shane ate his pizza and his cake. As they watched the movie, Edna couldn't help but be slightly bothered by Shane's manners. He smacked his lips and licked his fingers. *I can fix that,* Edna thought, and handed him her napkin. When Shane had finished his food, he placed his empty plate on the floor and fell asleep. His head rolled onto corner of the couch, and snores escaped his mouth in little puffs. *Aww. That's kind of cute,* Edna thought.

"Oh my God. Is he actually snoring?" Jenny asked, looking over her shoulder.

"I don't think he likes the movie," Edna's mom said, and they all laughed.

Just u n me?

Shane: nice seeing u! Srry I fel a sleep ☹

Edna: It was nice seeing you too. Where are you? At the hotel?

Shane: u r mch better looking irl than onlne

Edna: You are too! So cute!

Shane: m @ hotel i feel bad w/ ur mom paying

Edna: I'm sorry about my mom. She's just super protective of me ever since my dad died. Once she gets to know you she'll lighten up. On a positive note Jenny thinks you're cool (and cute).

Shane: nice 2 meet her i wish…

Edna: ????

Shane: i wish we cld hve more time u know just u n me?

Edna: Agreed. It would have been nice to talk to just you.

Shane: maybe someday huh?

Edna: Yeah, maybe someday.

Shane: u r gr8

Edna: You too.

Shane: i like u

Edna: I like you too.

Shane: …

Edna: … ?

Shane: i dn't know … imagined it turning out different

Edna: What do you mean?

Shane: us going out alone 2 maybe a candlelit dinner…

Edna: Shane you hardly have enough gas money for the trip home, and I'm broke. How would we be able to go out to a nice dinner?

Shane: i get it

Edna: Are you mad?

Shane: no m embarrassed stying in hotel 10 mls away iz not how i imagined it @ all tbh – itz kind of torture

Edna: Ohhh! That's so sweet. You shouldn't be embarrassed. I'm touched.

Shane: ur mom prob thinks m n idiot

Edna: My mom thinks everyone is an idiot. She's a softy. She'll warm up to you.

Shane: k so…?

Edna: ?

Shane: any chance me coming over after ur mom goes to bed n we can hang for a little? just u n me?

Edna: THAT is NOT a good idea. She'd KILL me if she found out. She might even call the police.

Shane: yeah no NOT b good 4 me no 5-O

Edna: 😊

Shane: wht time iz breakfast?

Edna: Technically we never eat breakfast together. It's kind of fend for yourself around here but I'm pretty sure Mom has something else in mind for tomorrow. She was thinking about 9:00? You can get here earlier if you want. I'll be up around 8:00. We could probably have some time just to talk and chill then.

Shane: kewl ill text u when up

Edna: Good night Shane! Thank you so much for coming all this way to spend my birthday with me!!!

Shane: my pleaz-ur! nite!

Young people are stupid

Edna sat at the kitchen table, staring out the window at the passing cars. She looked at her phone again, making sure she hadn't missed anything, making sure the ringer was on. It was 9:10 a.m. *He should've been there by now*, she thought.

"Did you text him?" her mother asked.

"Yes. I texted him," Edna snapped.

"Young lady, you had better adjust that tone. Do you understand?"

"Yes, Mom. I'm sorry. I'm just..."

"Anxious?"

"Yes."

"Nervous?"

"Yes."

"I get it. I'm sorry he's not here yet," Edna's mom said and came over and gave her a little hug.

"I told him he could get here at eight, so we could talk. I wonder if he's mad at me?"

"Mad? Why would he be mad?"

"Because he drove all the way out here, and we really didn't get to talk," Edna said, resting her chin on her palm.

"Edna, I hope you understand..."

"I understand, Mom. I don't blame you. I get it. I just wonder if he understands. His family is so different than ours."

"How so?"

"Well, they're a little more lenient than you," she said, picking up a napkin and twisting it around and around.

"Well..." her mom began.

"I'm not saying that's a good thing. By lenient, I mean that they don't really care what he does. I like that you care about me. I'm not blaming you," Edna said and checked her phone again. "Shall we eat?"

"Don't you want to wait?" Edna's mom asked.

"I don't know. I'm hungry. I wonder if he went home last night. Like, he couldn't sleep or something, and he just said, forget this. I'm out."

"Edna, you never know what could've happened. He could've slept through his alarm or been so tired that he forgot to even set one."

"You think I should call his room?" Edna asked.

"It couldn't hurt," her mom said.

Edna thumbed through her phone, looking for the phone number and called. "Hello, I was wondering if you could connect me to room 115? ... Oh he checked out? .... When? ... Okay. Thank you," Edna said and turned to her mom. "They said he just checked out. I'm going to try his phone again." As Edna was waiting for Shane to pick up, he pulled into their driveway. He popped out of the car, holding his phone above his head, pointing to it. Edna went to the door and held it open for him. He almost ran inside.

"I am so sorry. My phone ran out of power and my alarm didn't go off. I left the charger at home," he said and kissed Edna on the cheek. Edna blushed and glanced at her mom.

"Hello, Shane," Edna's mother said.

"Hello Mrs. Barrett."

"How'd you sleep?" she asked.

"Great. Thanks. And thank you again for the hotel room. I'm embarrassed that I didn't put a little more thought into coming out here."

"No problem. You're young, and young people are stupid."

"Mom! You can't talk to Shane like that…"

"Relax, Edna. I'm just kidding. Shane here knows I'm kidding, right?" she asked and smiled at Shane.

"Yes, Mrs. Barrett. I know you're joking." He blushed and looked at his shoes.

"Let's get your phone recharged," she said, pointing to the charger on the counter, "and get this breakfast started. What'll you have? Eggs? Toast? Eggos?"

"Yeah. I'd like some eggs, please. Scrambled."

"Three?" Edna's mother asked. Shane nodded. "Toast?" Shane nodded again. He sat down at the kitchen table across from Edna.

"How'd you sleep, Edna?" he asked.

"Fine."

"Shane," Mrs. Barrett said, her back to him as she worked over the stove. "What is it you do back in Chicago?"

"Well, I'm getting my GED online, just like Edna, that's how we met, and I'm cleaning buildings at night with my mom."

"Oh. Does your mom own a cleaning service?"

"No. She just got me the job."

"Mom, Shane wants to own his own business someday, don't you?" Edna said.

"Yes. I like working on cars, and my dream job would be to own a junkyard."

"Really?" Mrs. Barrett asked. "A junkyard?"

"Have you ever been to one?" he asked.

"Can't say as I have," she said, still processing the information.

"It's magical. You go early in the morning while the dew is still sitting on the old windshields, and the air is filled with a mixture of damp earth, rusted metal, and sunshine. You walk through the gate, and it's like a treasure hunt. You know what you need, so you walk around, looking for those vehicles. It's kind of like a scavenger hunt in a graveyard. Each of the vehicles has a history, you know. I'd love to own a junkyard."

"Well, you do sound very passionate about it."

"Yes, ma'am, I am."

The kitchen was filled the clinking of breakfast utensils on ceramic plates. The smell of coffee, eggs, and toast filled the room. Breakfast carried on with small talk and funny stories about Edna growing up. The bright room was filled with laughter and smiles.

"What time are you heading out?" Mrs. Barrett asked at a lull in the conversation.

"I should probably be heading home soon. I've gotta work tonight, seven to three," he said and stood up from the table.

"Ugh. Those hours suck," Edna said, following him to the door.

"Here," Mrs. Barrett said as she dug around in her purse. "Take this just in case you run into any trouble." She handed Shane two twenty-dollar bills.

"Oh, Mrs. Barrett, I can't take your money, especially after you made me this wonderful breakfast and paid for my hotel room last night."

"I insist," she said. She unrelentingly waved the folded bills at him until he took the money.

"I'll pay you back," he said and tucked the bills in his wallet. "I get paid next Friday. I'll send you the money."

"There's no need to pay me back, just promise me that you'll plan a little better the next time you take a trip anywhere," she said.

"I will," he said. "Goodbye, Edna. It was great to finally meet you in person," he said and hugged her. She squeezed him as tight as she could.

"It was very nice to meet you, too," she said once they let go. "Make sure you call me when you get home, or if you get bored while driving. Promise?"

"I promise," he said. He smiled as he backed out the front door and down the stoop. He turned and walked to his car. Edna could feel her eyes filling with tears. He turned back around and waved. Edna wiped her eyes with her sleeve and waved back.

"Call me," she yelled after him.

"I will," he yelled back.

Are you blind?

The wind blew the rain sideways, and it pelted the windows, making unusually loud sounds. Joe thought it was odd for rain to sound so violent. As he walked into the kitchen to get breakfast, his mother handed him a new, red leather covered Bible.

"It's just like mine," she said and smiled. He felt the weight of it in his hands and fingered the thin, gold-edged pages. He held it to his nose and flipped through, inhaling the crispness. He loved the smell of new books. His mother packed his lunch while he sat down and poured himself a bowl of cereal.

"Are you nervous?" his mother asked.

"No, I'm okay with everything," he said and shoveled the cereal into his mouth.

"You know, the kids at my school used to make fun of me," she said.

"Huh?" he mumbled.

"They did. I used to carry my Bible around with me, from class to class, on top of my books. If someone would ask me about it, I would see it as an opportunity to tell them about Jesus. I would witness to them right there, in the middle of the hallway. I was a missionary in my own school. I was God's warrior." She wiped up around the sink and seemed to have daydreamed herself back to a different time and place.

"That's why I gave you the Bible this morning," she said, snapping out of her daze. She put her hands on her hips, and then pointed to the Bible. "I was hoping you'd continue where I left off. You know, spread the word of God throughout your new school. You've been baptized now and are old enough to understand how important it is that we spread His word."

Joe had to force a smile, and thought, with dread, about carrying the Bible through the halls of his new school. He didn't want people to think he was a weirdo. His mom walked over and put his lunchbox inside his backpack. She hesitated for a moment, looked inside the backpack, and again, she seemed lost in thought. Only this time, she looked pained. Then Joe realized that she was probably hurt because he hadn't immediately placed the Bible into his backpack.

"Mother, you can go ahead and put the Bible in there too," Joe said, gesturing toward the pack, looking to her for approval. His mother smiled, rearranged his backpack, and carefully tucked the Bible inside.

When his mother went upstairs, he reached in and removed the Bible from his bag. He didn't want anyone catching even a *glimpse* of it on his first day of junior high, or ever, for that matter. He heard his mother coming down the stairs, and he slipped the Bible onto the bookshelf alongside the other books before his mother entered the room. *It'll have to do for now*, he thought. He planned on hiding it a little bit better when he got home from school. He walked over to the door, trying not to look guilty, and watched for the bus.

"I love you," his mother said, smiling as she entered the room.

"I love you too," he said.

"I'm praying that you have a blessed day."

"Thanks, Mom. Here's the bus." And with that, he left his mother and the Bible at home.

Things went well that morning. He enjoyed meeting new people and catching up with old friends from elementary school. He was able to find all his classes, and all his teachers seemed pretty cool. It was after lunch, which had been painless, that he heard his name broadcast over the intercom: *Joseph Dolsen, please come to the office. Joseph Dolsen to the office, please.* His heart boomed in his ears. He had never, in his entire life, been called to the office, and now, on the first day of junior high, they called him. *How awkward,* he thought.

As he hurried to the office, searching for a reason that the office might need to talk to him. Maybe it was paperwork or something, or maybe they didn't have his parents' phone number on file, or the work phone number for his father was missing, or ... *something.*

He was mortified when he rounded the corner and saw his mother standing tall on the other side of the office window. She was holding something tight to her chest. Joe opened the door and walked over to her. She handed him the red Bible.

“You wanted this, right?” she asked. He saw tears in her eyes.

“Mom—,” he started to explain as he took the Bible from her pale hands. She ignored him and wiped the tears from her eyes with her thumb. She walked to the door.

“I'll see you at home,” she said, not looking back. And then he blacked out. It wasn't because she embarrassed him. He blacked out because at that moment, an unquantifiable amount of anger overwhelmed him. At that moment, he realized that he was standing in the middle of his new school, on the first day, with a Bible that he didn't even want to bring to school in the first place.

He was sick of it. For years she had insisted that he be as devoted to God as she was. She wanted him to feel the same way about God that she did. If she sensed that his faith was waning, or that his belief was slipping, she would assail him with religious self-help books, tell him inspiring stories, force him to listen to spiritual music with her, make him read certain passages from the Bible, make him attend meetings at church, and so much more. Year after year of this was exhausting and frustrating. She wanted him to be someone he wasn’t. All he wanted to do was figure out who he was without her pushing him toward her God. Anger flooded his body like the water rushing from behind a cracked dam.

His eyes swiveled up inside his skull, and the last thing he heard was the distant echo of his head as he hit the tile floor. And then there was nothing, only white noise and blackness surrounding him. A strange sort of peace overcame him.

He woke to the soft sound of fluorescent lights buzzing. His mother was sitting beside the cot that he was laying on. She was busy twisting a tissue in her hands. The harsh, artificial light framed her face. Joe doubted he could navigate through the trouble he was in; it was too complex, so he lied.

"Mother," he whispered and reached for her, pretending he couldn't see her.

"I'm right here," she said and touched his probing hand. "What's wrong? Can you not see me? Are you blind?"

"I see God," he said and reached for the fluorescent light with his free hand.

Her hands recoiled to her chest. "God? Is He talking to you? What's He saying?" she asked.

"He's saying that he has special plans for me, and that you should remember that, one day, I'll be in a position of great power." Then he pretended to pass out again. He laid there with his eyes shut and listened to her hurried breathing.

"Is everything all right over there?" the nurse asked from the corner of the office. Joe fought hard to keep from laughing.

"We're fine," his mother replied. "We're just going to head home after he comes to."

"He should see a doctor," the nurse said. "You need to take him to an acute-care center or an emergency room."

"Yes," his mother said. "We'll head to the ER from here, after he comes to."

***

In the car, his mother asked, "Do you remember our conversation in the nurse's office?"

"What are you talking about?" Joe asked. "I remember you brought me the Bible and that's it."

"Really?" She sat quiet for a moment and stared at the street unfolding ahead. "Well, the nurse wants me to take you to the ER because you passed out." Joe could feel her eyes on him, waiting for his reaction. "I'm just going to take you home to rest. Are you okay with that?"

"Sure. I guess so," Joe said, happy to not be in school.

"To be honest with you, I think your blackouts are a gift from God. I know I've told you that, but I just ... well, you're going to be great someday. I believe that you're with Him when you blackout. A doctor's not going to find anything wrong with you, because it's God's doing." The car fell silent. "Besides, your father would kill me if we had to pay for an unnecessary ER visit."

I'll call the police

For the first few hours after Shane left, Edna walked around the house in a daze. She couldn't focus on anything. She plopped down on her bed, exhausted, wanting to take a nap. She looked around her room at the posters on her walls and the trinkets on her dresser and shelves. They all seemed so silly, so immature now; now that she looked at everything through Shane's eyes. *What would Shane think of that? Would he think this was stupid?*

Everything around the room reminded her of him, too. She put on her favorite playlist and somehow, every song brought her back to him. Even songs about a guy cheating on his girlfriend reminded her of him: *Oh, Shane would never do anything like that,* she thought. Her thoughts became unbearable. She wondered how he was doing, driving back to Chicago. She picked up the phone and called. "How's the trip going?" she asked.

"Good," he said. "It's a little boring."

"You know what?"

"What?"

"I miss you," she said and smiled.

"I miss you, too," he said.

"You know what I've been thinking about all morning?" Edna asked.

"No. What?"

"I've been thinking about spending time with just you. No Jenny. No Mom. Just you."

"Ohhh yeah," Shane said. "I've thought about that, too. A lot."

"Would you kiss me?" she asked.

"Hell yeah!" he said.

Edna's heart surged at the thought. She imagined touching the side of his face with the tips of her fingers and pulling him near, touching her lips to his. "When do you think we could see each other again?" she asked.

"I'm off next weekend," he said. "I could shoot up there on Friday after work.

"I think I'd like that."

"Where would I stay?"

"Let me talk to Mom and see what I can do. Okay?" she asked, twirling her hair.

"Okay! Sounds good!"

"Call me when you get home," she said. "Or if you just wanna talk to pass the time."

"Yup. Will do," he said and hung up the phone.

Edna couldn't stop thinking about Shane. She started reading and rereading his texts and emails. She feared that she might look clingy, and despite her better judgement, she sent him text message after text message. He didn't reply. She worried that he had been in a terrible car accident, and that the next time she would see him was when he was lying in a casket in a funeral home somewhere outside of Chicago.

And then, in an attempt to counteract her dire premonitions, she thought through every possible situation in which his nonresponse could be logically explained: *He was driving and wouldn't want to text and drive; his phone battery had run out again; he was eating at McDonalds; he was so tired that he pulled over to take a nap; he was listening to his music way too loud and hadn't even realized that a text came in; he was...* It was exhausting.

She heard her mom come back from work. She put her phone down and walked out to the kitchen.

"Hi, honey," her mom said.

"Hi, Mom."

"What've you been up to all day?" she asked. "Did you finish your schoolwork?"

"Honestly, Mom, I didn't even look at it," she said and plopped down at a seat at the kitchen table.

"You didn't? Why not? Are you feeling oaky?"

"I don't know. Maybe I'm feeling a little down."

"Since Shane left this morning?"

"Yeah."

"You really like him, huh?"

"Yeah. I like him more than I thought I did. Just seeing him made me... Well, I know I miss him now more than I did before his visit."

"Can you call him?"

"He's not answering my calls or my texts..."

"And that bothers you, too?"

"Yeah," Edna said and took a napkin from its holder and began twisting it.

"Oh, honey, he'll get in touch with you. Remember, just this morning you were worried about him not returning your calls or texts or whatever and his phone had just died. You worry too much. Relax. Maybe his phone is dead again."

"I know ... Can I ask you a question?" Edna said, tearing the paper napkin into little pieces.

"Yeah. Sure. Shoot," her mom said, pulling out a chair and sitting down across the table from Edna.

"How would you feel about Shane coming back to spend some time with us – with me?"

"I mean, I guess I'd be okay with it. I'd like it if it were planned out next time, you know. He can't just stop by whenever he wants. It's not like he lives next door."

"Would you be okay with him staying here? When he visited?"

"Oh, honey, I don't know. I hardly know the kid, and can I be honest?" Edna's mom looked down at her hands in her lap.

"Uh-oh. No good conversation has ever started with, *Can I be honest*. What? Let me guess. You don't like him?"

"Well, I wouldn't exactly put it like that. I'm not sure that he's the kind of guy I see you with, you know, long term. I see you with someone with a little more character, a little more charisma. He just seems to be there. Blah. You know what I mean?"

"Mother. He is a very nice guy. He probably just *sat* there because he was scared of you. He didn't want to say anything wrong. You have to understand that he comes from a pretty messed up family."

"Yes. Yes. You said that. I'm not sure that's a good thing, either. He hasn't had good examples to model a relationship after."

"Mom, he's a really good guy. He doesn't need good role models. He knows what *not* to do and how *not* to treat people because he hated being treated that way. That's how he's learned to be a good boyfriend."

"He's your boyfriend now?"

"Well, no, not exactly. Not even close. We're just friends."

"You're definitely heading toward boyfriend/girlfriend status here, though."

"Really, Mom? I don't think so…"

"Edna, he drove hundreds of miles to surprise you on your birthday. You guys are heading toward a relationship."

"Whatever," Edna said, tearing the already shredded napkin into smaller pieces.

"Denial ain't just a river in Egypt, honey," her mom said and got up from the chair and pushed it into the table.

"So…?" Edna asked.

"So … what?" her mom asked.

"So, can he come visit?"

"Sure, as long as he has somewhere to stay," she said, leaning her hip against the chair.

"He can't stay here? He could sleep on my bed, and I could sleep on the couch."

"That sounds like a bad idea to me."

"How about I sleep on the floor in your room?"

"How about I'm not interested in being woken up by you every time you come in and out of the room. I've gotta work. Who's going to chaperone you guys when I'm at work?"

"I'm eighteen. We don't need a chaperone. Besides, you've been leaving me home alone since I was twelve. I can take care of myself. Plus, Shane would be added safety."

"Um, no!"

"That's your final answer? Don't you want to think about it?"

"I'll think about it, but I'll be honest with you, I don't see my mind changing," and with that, her mom walked out of the room.

Edna spent the evening floating around the house like a ghost. She went into the family room where her mom reclined in her La-Z-Boy, eating microwave-popcorn from the bag and watching a movie. Edna sat down on the couch next to her and began fidgeting with the cover on the arm of the couch.

"What's up Edna?" her mom asked.

"Nothing," she said. "I'm just trying to figure out what to do."

"Is your schoolwork done?"

"I can do it tomorrow," she said, staring blankly at the arm cover she was rolling between her fingers.

"Well, if you're looking for something to do, why don't you do that?"

"It's a group project, and my partner is sick, so I'm just going to wait for her to get better."

"Edna..." her mom said, putting the popcorn bag down on her lap.

"What?"

"You have to stop moping around here. Do something. You're driving me crazy."

"I'm worried. I still haven't heard from him."

"Edna," her mom said, putting her movie on pause. "You need to chill out. You're assuming the worst, here. There's no need for that. Go to bed or something. Why don't you sit down and watch this movie with me? It's super cheesy, but it'll suck you in."

"Mom? Really? I'm worried about Shane..."

"I'm sure he's fine, Edna. Sit down and watch."

"I'll pass," she said.

Her mom un-paused her movie.

Edna meandered back to her room where she flipped open her laptop and began searching for signs of Shane. She checked the online class to see if he'd logged in or not: nothing. She checked his social media accounts: nothing. Then she began scanning the route from Minnesota to Chicago, and she clicked on every red or yellow slowing of traffic to see if it was an accident, or if it was construction. If it was an accident, she would then try to find the town that it was in, and she would try to find the police scanner for that town online, and then she'd listen in for clues or signs of Shane. Then there was a knock on her door. "Come in," she said.

"I'm going to bed," her mom said as she stepped into the room.

"What time is it?"

"It's almost 10:30," her mom said.

"Wow! Where'd the time go?"

"Dunno. I just wanted to say good night and check in on you."

"Good night," Edna said.

"Have you heard from Shane?" her mom asked.

"Nope," Edna said, turning her attention back to her computer.

"Well. I hope everything works out, sweetheart, and if it doesn't then there's something better in store for you."

"Really?" Edna asked, a little put out that her mom would mention Shane and her not working out.

"I love you," her mom said, as she turned to exit the room.

"I love you, too," Edna said just before her mom pulled the door shut.

Edna looked at the glowing screen, and the energy that had, moments ago, fueled her search for Shane turned into weariness. She was hit with the scope and silliness of the search. Her eyes became heavy; she shut her computer and set it on her bedside stand. She checked her phone, plugged it in to the charger, and shut the light off. She closed her eyes and began willing herself to sleep.

All she could think about was Shane. She began counting numbers, imagining their black shapes as she said them in her mind, starting over every time an errant thought snuck into her head. She tried blinking her eyes one hundred times, hoping that that exercise would make her eyes heavy, and as a result, she'd fall asleep. She tried to imagine herself on a beach on a warm day. Nothing would clear her head. Sleep was her enemy.

She sat up in bed and looked around. Her mouth felt dry, so she went into the kitchen to get some water. She wanted to sleep; her eyes were heavy with weariness. She went back to her room and changed into an oversized t-shirt and her most comfortable sleeping shorts. She slid between her cool sheets and smiled at the luxurious feeling of sleep slowly creeping through her mind and freezing her frenzied thoughts that had galloped freely through her head all day.

Just as she was about to sleep, she thought she heard a gentle tapping, tapping on her bedroom window. She laid there and listened. *Surly it was just a branch falling outside, or a distant sound that had mutated into something else on its way to my ear,* Edna thought. Her heart began to beat rapidly as she wondered if it was Shane. She jumped up from her bed and ran across the thick carpet. She pulled her blinds up and squinted past the reflections of her room, trying to make out the shrubs and trees that she knew were in the yard just outside of her first-floor window. It took her eyes a moment to adjust and see past the reflection of the room. Then she saw Shane's face outlined in the darkness. He was on the other side of the glass. At first, she was startled. He smiled and waved. She waved back. She stared at him; her mind scrambling to catch up with the events. Shane made a gesture for her to open the window. Edna fumbled with the window fastener and, with all her might, pulled the reluctant window open. "What the hell?" she asked. "What are you doing here?"

"I got halfway home and realized that I didn't want to go home. I just wanted to be with you, so I turned around and drove back," he said, his hands on his thighs, leaning in toward the window.

"Why didn't you answer any of my texts?" she asked. "I've been worried sick about you for hours."

Shane smiled and shrugged his shoulders. "I thought about texting you, but at the half-way point, when I decided to turn around, I knew that I'd have to lie to you if I did, and I knew you'd be all like, 'Where are you now?' and shit, and

I didn't want to lie. I didn't want you to try to talk me out of driving back, either." He looked at her. "You would've right? Tried to talk me out of driving back here?"

Edna smiled. "Yeah. You're probably right," she said. She realized that she'd never been this happy her whole life. It felt good to be wanted, especially by someone she liked so much. "What now?" she asked.

"I don't know. I've been sitting in my car on the street in front of your house all evening, hoping you'd leave to get something, so we could talk. I saw that your mom was home, and I didn't want to show up unannounced again. I don't think she'd be cool with that."

"Yeah. Good call," Edna said, looking over her shoulder at the mention of her mom.

"Are you going to let me in?" he asked, moving closer to the window. Edna stepped back and studied the screen. She fumbled with the latches until it popped out. Shane caught it. He leaned the screen against the house and climbed into Edna's room. She shut the window once he was in there. He pulled her to him and kissed her for the first time. A flood of emotions exploded through her body. The tiny blond hairs on her arms stood on end.

"Wait," she said when they came up for air.

"What?" Shane asked. "What's wrong?"

"How's this going to work?"

"What do you mean?"

"I mean, we have to be quiet. My mom's not going to let you stay. We need to come up with a plan or something.

She's not expecting you until next weekend. She'll get all weird if she finds out you turned around."

"I can stay in my car at night and come in the house to eat and clean up while she's at work."

"I'm not crazy about that idea," Edna said.

"Why not?" Shane asked.

"Well, I don't like all of the sneaking around. I don't really want to lie to my mom, and besides, the neighbors talk. They're terrible gossips."

"Oh. Really? Okay," Shane said. He pulled a pack of cigarettes from his pocket and started smacking them against the palm of his hand. "Do you want one?"

"No thank you. I didn't know you smoked," she said, her head tilted to the side.

"Since I was like 12," he said and pulled one out of the soft pack. He plugged it into his mouth, and it dangled there. "I've tried to quit," he said, the cigarette bouncing with every word spoken. "It's a bad habit. I'll quit if it bothers you."

"Oh. Okay," she said, feeling a little uneasy, hoping that this was the last of the surprises. "But you can't smoke in here. Mom will kill me."

"I drive all this way, and I can't smoke a cigarette?" he asked, cigarette emphatically bobbing up and down in his mouth.

"At least smoke by the window, or climb out the window and smoke out there," Edna said, and pointed. A confluence of emotions swirled around inside. Every-other thump of her heart was filled with excitement at the thrill of doing something she shouldn't; the opposite heartbeats were filled with the fear and anxiety that comes with not being able to control a situation.

Shane took her desk chair, sat it next to the window and opened it. He pulled a lighter from his pocket and lit the cigarette. He blew most of the smoke out the window, but the errant wisps that curled around themselves on the way up to her celling made her panic. "Shane, please make sure all of the smoke gets out the window."

"Relax, babe. It's not going to be a problem," he said. He moved from the chair to the windowsill and leaned farther out when he exhaled. "There. Is that better? Does that make you happy?"

"Yes. Thank you," she said, not liking his tone.

There was a knock on the door. "Yes," Edna said.

"Edna are you smoking in there?" her mother asked from the other side of the door. "It smells like smoke in my room, and..." She stopped speaking when she opened the door and saw Shane smoking at the windowsill. "What the hell is going on, Edna?" she asked, turning from Shane to Edna.

"Shane decided to come back."

"And what? He snuck in through the window? He didn't want to knock? What the hell?" her mom said, staring at Edna.

"Mom. Really. I had no idea he was coming back. He just knocked on my window a few minutes ago," Edna said.

"Is this why you've been acting so strange all day? Were you planning this?"

"Excuse me, Ms. Barrett, perhaps I can explain..."

"You need to leave immediately, or I'll call the police," she said.

"Mom, really, you're overreacting," Edna said.

"He's bad news. He doesn't care about rules. Look at him, sitting there, smoking, showing up at my house twice, both times unannounced. This is ridiculous. What kind of person does this?"

"I'm in love," Shane said. "I love your daughter, and that's why I've been acting so crazy."

"Oh. Jesus, Shane. How old are you? 19?" Edna's mother asked.

"Yes, ma'am," he said.

"You aren't in love. You hardly know Edna, and Edna hardly knows you."

"Mom, please. Can we just talk about this?" Edna asked.

"No. We can't. Not at 11:30 on a worknight. Shane, you need to leave. Now!" Edna's mom yelled and turned to leave the room.

"Where's she going?" Shane asked.

"I don't know," Edna said. Her mom came back with her phone in her hand.

"I'm going to call the police if you don't leave immediately," she said and began dialing.

"Mom. Please. He doesn't have anywhere to go?"

"He can go home. I gave him gas money to go home. He needs to go home. I'm calling now," she said. "Nine," she said loudly and deliberately pressed the button. "One."

"Mom! If he goes, I'm leaving, too. The least you can do is let him stay here for the night, and then he'll leave in the morning."

"It'll be a cold day in hell when I let that boy stay in my house. I don't even know him, and what I do know, I don't like. You don't know anything about him, either," she said.

"I know that I love him," she said and looked to Shane. He smiled.

"Shane. You need to leave now," Edna's mom said, her finger hovering above the last one on the phone.

"Fine. I get it. I'm out of here," he said and climbed out the window. He leaned back in and said, "Edna. I'll be waiting in my car if you'd like to join me on my trip back to Chicago. My mom would *love* to have you visit."

"Let me pack a few things," Edna said and walked over and kissed him.

"Get the hell off of my property!" Edna's mom shouted.

"I get it. I'm leaving. I'm leaving," Shane said and raised his hands over his head like he was a prisoner surrendering and walked away. "I'll be waiting, Edna," he called over his shoulder. He took a long drag from his cigarette and flicked the butt toward the house. It exploded like a small orange firework when it hit the siding.

"Pick that up!" Edna's mother yelled after him. He waved her off, mumbled something under his breath, and walked to his car.

Edna changed into jeans, grabbed her backpack, dumped everything out, and manically began packing.

"Edna, please don't go. He's bad news. Trust me. I know the type."

"Let him stay then," she pleaded. "Then I don't have to go anywhere."

"Edna, my job is to take care of you, even if it means tough love. I won't go against my gut on this one. He's got issues. I don't want you going off with him."

"I'm eighteen, mom. I can do whatever I want," Edna said as she grabbed her phone charger and computer and slid them into her backpack.

"Please, Edna. Please, this is not what I want for you. You don't know if this guy's a serial killer or a rapist or something horrible like that..."

"Mom, Shane and I have talked every day for months, sometimes more than once a day. I know him. I wish you'd give him a chance," she said as she flung her backpack over her shoulder.

"Edna. Please!"

"Seriously, Mom. You're being ridiculous! Why can't you just treat me like an adult? Why can't I just go to the car and ask him to come back, and he could stay for a couple days? You could get to know him."

"I don't want that man inside my house. You saw how disrespectful he was to me," she said and pointed out the window. "He threw a lit cigarette against my house and refused to pick up the butt. God only knows what he called me under his breath."

"Please, Mom. He's angry."

"And why is he angry?"

"Because you threatened to call the cops on him," Edna said, stamping her foot. "that's why he's angry."

"He's angry because he can't run roughshod over me. He's angry because he can't get what he wants. I'm in the way…"

"And what, exactly, does that mean?" Edna asked.

Silence…

"Are you talking about *sex*?" Edna asked.

"God, Edna! How can you be so blind? That guy's bad news! Deep down, you know it, too. Listen to me. Listen to that little voice inside..."

"You're just jealous," Edna said, her arms crossed, and her jaw set.

"Jealous of what? That?" she said and pointed out the window.

"You're jealous that I have someone, and you don't."

"Oh please," Edna's mother said and crossed her arms.

"You're jealous that I have someone who is *alive,*" Edna said, wanting her words to hurt.

"What exactly does that mean?" her mom asked.

"I'm just saying ... Never mind," Edna said. She stared at her mom. Edna walked toward her, determined to push past her if necessary. Her mom stepped aside. She thought she saw tears in her mom's eyes as she passed. A twinge of regret oozed into her consciousness, and then she thought of Shane, and the anger that had fueled her hurtful words returned, pushing any sort of regret out. She walked out the front door. The sun-dried grass crunched underfoot in the dark as she walked across the lawn to Shane's car.

"Ready?" he asked as she got into the car.

"Let's go," she said and fastened her seatbelt.

I know what it's like to be dead

For the most part, Joe loved their family walks. The entire family would pile into the car, drive to a different part of town, or a nearby town, and look at old houses. He liked the warm, yellow glow that emanated from house windows in the early evening, and he liked listening to his mother and father dream together. It gave him a much-needed sense of security … most of the time.

They would say things like, *Maybe we should sell our house and buy this one. Sure, it needs a lot of work, but think of the things we could do with an old, beautiful shell like that.* Occasionally, Jessica and Joe would get in on the dreaming by expressing their preference for one house over the other or by calling dibs on certain bedroom windows. They would usually stop at McDonald's on the way home for a soda or hot cocoa, depending on the weather.

One time, after they all piled in the car, Joe's father held up a cassette tape, so they could see it in the backseat. He had loosened up over the years regarding music and had been bringing home different rock-n-roll CDs for the entire family to listen to. Joe thought it was a passive-aggressive resistance to his mother's growing rigidity. His mother had wondered, on occasion, if his father was having an affair, and the new music he was listening to was inspired by whichever woman he was currently seeing on the side.

"What is it?" Jessica asked.

"It's the Beatles' album, *Revolver*," he said. "I picked it up at lunch today." He pushed it into the player. "I know it's old, but it's supposed to be a classic." They drove toward the low-hanging winter sun. The song *She Said, She Said* was playing when they arrived at their destination. His father waited until the song was completely over before he shut the car off, as was his habit. Everyone ambled out of the car into the cold and put on their hats, scarves, and gloves. They walked under the streetlight glow.

"Isn't this invigorating?" his father asked, inhaling the winter air.

"I know what it's like to be dead," Joe's mother said. Everyone stopped and looked at her. "Like the song we were just listening to."

The small tribe paused, and everyone absorbed the information. After his father moved forward, they all followed and continued to walk. The only sound was the crunching of snow under foot. Joe imagined they were walking on eggshells. A familiar sense of dread creeped into his heart; it happened every time his mother began one of her rants, and this had all the makings of a rant.

"So, what exactly does that mean, *You know what it's like to be dead*?" Father asked, breaking the unnerving silence. His words formed clouds that hung in the frozen air and then drifted off toward the edge of the streetlight where they then dissipated into the darkness.

"Being married to you is like a spiritual death, so I know what it's like to be dead," Joe's mother said. "I feel dead inside, that's what I mean." She shoved her hands deep into her jacket pockets.

"Really?" Joe's father asked. The air left his body. His broad shoulders lost their angle.

"I had a dream last night," his mother said, as she re-tied her wool scarf around her head.

"Another dream?" his father asked. "Let me guess, it was from God?"

"As a matter of fact, it was." She continued walking. "He showed me many things in my dream." She stared down at the sidewalk. Each step was inline, deliberate, and succinct.

"Really? What'd he show you this time?"

"He showed me a beautiful house in Key West, Florida, and he promised that it would be my reward for my faith and for following his will." She looked up at Joe's father as she said this. Joe watched for his father's reaction.

"Well," his father said, "I'm not sure what you want me to do with that."

"I need to quit working and write my story," Joe's mother said. "That's how I'm going to be successful. My journals, tracing my walk with God, *will* be published, and I *will* be rewarded with riches."

"God showed you this?" his father asked. "Did he show you how we're supposed to pay the bills while you're not working, while you're writing?"

"I knew you wouldn't understand. I knew this was going to be a problem," she said. "That's why, in my dream, it was just the kids and I at the beach house in Florida."

Joe's father said nothing. He turned around and walked back to the car. Joe's mother followed but didn't bother keeping her husband's pace. Jessica and Joe trailed them both in cold silence. They all climbed into the car. Joe knew better than to ask for hot chocolate.

As his father drove, Joe pressed his forehead against the cold car window and watched the neighborhood Christmas lights blur by.

"Joseph," his mother said from the front seat.

"Yes?" he said.

"You know what it's like to speak with God, don't you?"

He remained silent.

"The next time you blackout, could you verify my dream with Him, and then tell your father that it's true?"

He looked at her and thought he could see her thoughts swirling around behind her eyes, waiting for him to validate her beliefs. He could see his father's shoulders tense up, waiting for words to fall from his mouth. He didn't know what to do, so he pretended to blackout.

"Oh my, he's passed out," he heard his mother say. "Pull over, pull over," she yelled at his father. Joe sat there, his head against the car window, enjoying the silence until he thought he could feel everyone in the car watching him. He opened his eyes. His father stared at him in the rear-view mirror. His mother had twisted around in the front seat, now facing him.

“Well?” she asked.

“Well, what?”

“Well, what'd God say?”

“I got nothing, Mom,” he said. “Sorry. I didn't see God this time.”

She turned back around.

“What's God look like anyway?” Jessica asked. Joe couldn't tell if she was screwing with him or not.

“He looks like light,” Joe said flatly and stared out the window.

His father ejected the Beatles CD from the player, rolled down his window, and threw the disc, like a frisbee, out into the cold night. Joe watched it disappear into a snow drift along the ditch.

A vending machine in the bathroom

Shane and Edna drove across the Midwest from Norwood, Minnesota toward Chicago via I94 and I90. Edna was fascinated by the horizon. She imagined the clouds overhead to be a gray-cloud blanket, and she and Shane were driving the car between the blanket and its earth mattress. It felt warm and cozy. As the trip wore on, however, the excitement faded into apprehension and, the farther away she went, it became fear.

"Shane, you're going to have to convince me that this is the right thing to do," she said, staring out at the rolling farmland that flew by the passenger window.

"Edna, we owe it to our relationship to do this. Besides, you're an adult. You can make your own decisions."

"Yeah. I am an adult, right?" She smiled and felt a warmth spread inside when Shane called what they had a relationship.

"Yeah. And we would've stayed there if she hadn't been such a bitch about it," he said, stepping on the gas as he pulled around a semi-truck.

"She's not a bitch," Edna said, pulling out her phone, checking for messages.

"Well, you know what I mean. She can act like a bitch without being a bitch, right?"

Edna shrugged and texted her mom: *Mom. I'm sorry. I love you and will be back soon. I hope you understand.*

"Who are you texting?" Shane asked, looking over at her phone.

"My mom," she said, nonchalantly.

"What? Are you telling her that I called her a bitch?" Shane asked.

"No. Not at all. I just told her that I was sorry and that I loved her."

"Bullshit!" Shane exploded, slamming his palm on the steering wheel.

"No honestly, that's what I texted. Look," Edna said and handed her phone to Shane.

Shane read. "So, what exactly are you sorry for? Sorry for leaving with me? Sorry for what, exactly?" he asked.

"I don't know. I'm sorry I left on such bad terms. I said some hurtful things to her that I'd like to take back. She's my mom and I don't really want to hurt her."

"I guess I get it," Shane said, handing the phone back to her. "I'm sorry I snapped. I wanna be in your life for a long time, and I don't want bad blood between your mom and me," Shane said. "I'm sorry I called your mom a bitch. I know she's not. She's just looking out for you. She doesn't know me yet. That's hard for me, ya know? To have someone I want to impress and to like me, but she doesn't. She thinks the worst of me."

"She'll see that you're a good guy," Edna said and ran her fingers through Shane's hair. Shane smiled. Edna was relieved that he was no longer upset. She didn't want to be the source of his unhappiness.

"I need to stop and use the bathroom," she said, digging in her backpack for her little purse.

"Sure. We'll get off here and fill up," he said and exited the interstate. They pulled into a truck stop, parked, and went into the store.

He was waiting for her when she came out. She plopped into the car seat, leaned over and kissed him. He grabbed the back of her head and returned her kiss.

"Should we go somewhere a little more private?" he asked.

"What do you mean?"

"I mean, I got this from a vending machine in the bathroom," he said and held up a condom package. Initially, it didn't register with Edna what it was, so she leaned forward to read the packaging. Shane laughed.

"What? You've never seen one of these before?"

"No. I mean, I know what it is … I guess. I've just never seen one this close," she leaned back against the passenger door and thought about what was happening.

"Are you a … virgin?"

"No... Well, to be honest, yes. Honestly though, I'm not sure I'm ready for this. I always imagined my first time being something special, you know, not in a car."

"You mean not in a car with *me*?" Shane asked.

"No. I've thought about you and this moment plenty. I just never imagined it would be in a car."

"Oh," Shane said. He turned the key and the engine roared to life. He threw the car into reverse. The tires squealed as he tore out of the parking spot. Edna's head jerked forward. Her seatbelt caught. Then, Edna was thrown back in her seat when he slammed the car in drive and ripped out of the parking lot, tires spinning and grinding across the gravel covered pavement, screeching when they hit the road.

"Shane!" Edna yelled. "What are you doing?"

"I'm taking you home," he said as they pulled away from the gas station onto the frontage road.

"My home, or your home?" she asked.

"I'm taking you back to your home," he said.

"Why?" she asked, confused. "Because I didn't want to have sex with you in your car?"

"Yes ... No ... I don't know," he said and cast a side glance at her as he drove.

"It's not that I don't want to have sex with you. I just don't want my first time to be in a car at a gas station in Wisconsin. Surely, you can respect that, right?"

"I guess so," he said and pulled the car to the side of the road. "My feelings were just hurt, you know, when you didn't want to have sex with me."

"That's not what I said. I just don't want it to happen in a car. It'll happen, baby," she said and stroked his hair again. "Now, take me to your place," she said. Shane set the condom in the compartment under the radio. Edna stared at it all the way to Chicago. The irreversibility of the situation exhausted her. She surrendered herself to the hum of the wheels and engine and the radio, the white noise of travel, and she fell asleep.

These offices don't clean themselves

Edna followed Shane through the parking lot between two identical apartment buildings. The atmosphere was stale and hot and compact. The smell of drying laundry hung in the warm air. She heard the low murmurs of conversations spilling from open apartment windows. She threw her bag over her shoulder and almost had to run to keep up with Shane. He climbed the stairs, two at a time, put his key in the apartment door, and opened it. He stood aside to let her in.

"Welcome to my castle," he said, bowing and making a grand gesture. "Well, actually it's my mom's apartment. I'll show you my room after I introduce you to her." He stepped inside. "Mom? Mom," he called. Edna looked around at the small, outdated living room and kitchen.

"Shane. Where the fuck have you been?" his mom yelled from another room.

"Mom come in here. I've got someone I'd like you to meet," he said. Edna thought his voice lacked confidence, and it worried her. His mom rounded the corner, drying her long dark hair with a green towel. She was short, and Edna thought that she had probably been considered beautiful at one point in her life, but now, what looked like anger was etched into the lines of her face.

"Who's this? And where the hell have you been? I had to lie for you at work."

"This is Edna. She's my girlfriend," he said. Edna stepped forward for a possible hug or at the very least a handshake. Shane's mom gave her a curt nod, nothing more.

"She's the reason you bailed on work without telling anyone?"

"Yeah. I drove up to Minnesota to be with her on her birthday. I thought I told you that?"

His mother shrugged. "You'd better get ready for work. These offices don't clean themselves," she said and left the room.

"Sorry. She's got no social game," he said. "Follow me. I'll show you my room." They walked down the narrow hallway, past the open bathroom where his mother was leaning over the sink, looking in the mirror, putting on eyeliner. He opened the door to his room. There was nothing on his walls, no posters, nothing. His mattress was on the floor, and an old milk crate served as his bedside stand. His clothes were strewn across the room. "Sorry," he said as he picked his clothes off his bed and threw them in a corner. "I had no idea that things would work out this way, otherwise I would've cleaned up, you know?" He blushed. "Sit here," he said and patted the bed. She cautiously sat down. He sat next to her and leaned in for a kiss.

"Um, Shane," she said, putting her hand on his chest, leaning away from him, so she didn't have to push him away.

"What's wrong?" he asked.

“You’re mom’s in the next room.”

“Yeah?”

“I’m not sure I’m comfortable…”

“Oh. Relax. You don’t have anything to worry about. She’s more like a roommate than anything.” He leaned in again, lips leading the way.

“I’m still not comfortable,” she said, this time pushing him back a little, worried that he would become upset with her resistance. “Please try to understand. I’m not comfortable here,” she said, instantly regretting her word choice. “Just give me time,” she said, reassuringly. Just then there was a knock on the door.

“Shane. Shane. We have to leave,” his mother yelled from the other side of the door. “We’ll be late if we don’t leave now.” He opened the door. “Is she staying?” his mother asked, fiddling with a headband, pointing at Edna with her elbow.

“Yes,” Shane said. He turned to Edna, “I have to go, or they’ll fire me,” he said. “Help yourself to anything in the refrigerator. We’ll be back around 3:30 this morning.” He reached out and touched her chin and smiled. “You can sleep here,” he said and pointed to his bed.

Edna heard the door to the apartment shut. Their voices faded, and she exhaled. She realized that she had been on edge for hours, and this was the first moment that was hers; the first moment that she could control. She laid on the mattress on her side and pulled her knees to her chest. Somewhere in her head she knew her circumstances could be changed, and that big decisions should be made, could be made, were being made, even by not making them. There were so many thoughts swirling around in her head, and, at that moment, she longed for some sort of life preserver. She was disappointed that Shane's mother had not welcomed her like he said she would. She felt like Shane had lied to her. *Maybe she's just in a bad mood?* she thought. She feared things were spinning out of control and was overwhelmed and incapable of sorting through everything. All she wanted to do was sleep – surrender to the nothingness that sleep offered. Escape. She felt as if her blood were muddied with sand, with sadness, bogging her heart down. She shut her eyes, and a tear rolled down her cheek; it surprised her because she hadn't given herself permission to feel anything, especially sadness.

I know you're not really sleeping

Edna woke up, sat on the mattress in Shane's room and looked around. She leaned over the milk crate that his bedside lamp sat on. There was nothing else there. No books. No magazines. Only a phone charger and some socks were around the milk crate. She stood up and walked around his room. She opened his closet and stuck her head in. There was a backpack on the floor and what looked like winter clothes folded and stacked on a shelf. There were a couple of button-down shirts hanging in there, but nothing else.

Edna was thirsty, so she walked to the kitchen, opened a cupboard, and got a plastic McDonald's cup from the shelf. She filled it with water and drank it down in one prolonged sip. She felt like a sponge absorbing water. She put the cup in the sink and opened the refrigerator. There was nothing remarkable in it: milk, juice, produce, plastic containers, etc. She shut the door and opened the freezer on top. Again, normal findings except for a large bottle of Absolute vodka. She took it out and examined it. She noticed that her warm fingers were leaving frozen imprints on the bottle. "Oh shit," she muttered. She took the bottle to the sink and rinsed her frozen fingerprints off before returning it to the freezer.

She casually walked around the kitchen and perused the envelopes and bills that were strewn out across the counter, but she didn't pick them up and examine them. She didn't think that was right. *Money is a private thing,* she thought. She looked out the kitchen window and saw a dull glow in the sky. She stepped out the back door onto the little balcony and looked up. She was surprised by the unnatural light that lit the sky. To her, the illumination looked like a dirty light dome. There were no stars. She couldn't see the moon, just a dreary purple-yellow glow. *This is nothing like back home,* she thought. She heard noises coming from the balcony below her and hurried back inside.

She walked into the family room. The first thing she noticed was the outdated furniture and décor. It was like she had stepped back into the 1990s. She looked at the montage of framed pictures hanging on the wall. She wondered if she'd ever get to meet the family members in the pictures. She recognized photos of a young Shane, stopped and smiled.

She saw the TV remote on the coffee table. She sat down. The plaid couch was covered with a rough fabric, almost like a burlap. She turned on the TV and flipped the channel to an old episode of Friends. She laughed a few times and fell asleep. She woke up later to a black-and-white TV show that she didn't recognize. *What time is it?* she wondered. *Surely, they aren't home yet. They would've woken me up, right?.* She listened. Nothing. Groggy, she went to the bathroom and washed her face. She went back into Shane's room, shut the light off and fell back asleep.

Edna woke to an arm snaking around her waist. She laid there paralyzed, sorting through the sleep fog in her brain. *Where am I? Whose arm is this?*

"Hey, baby," Shane whispered in her ear. He was so close that it would've tickled if she had been in a different state of mind. She pretended she was asleep. "Hey, it's me," he whispered and pulled her hair away from her face and began kissing her neck. She grunted and pushed him away, still pretending to sleep. "My mom's out at her boyfriend's place, so we don't have to worry about that," he said and continued to kiss her neck. "I know you're not really sleeping." She rolled over and opened her eyes.

"Shane, please, I'm so tired. This isn't how I'd imagined it. Can we please wait?" she said and propped her head up on her hand.

"I mean … sure … I guess so," he said and rolled on his back.

"I'm sorry. I just…"

"What? You just don't like me?" he asked. "I mean, I drive hundreds of miles to be with you, and you treat me like this…" The anger in his voice scared her. She had never known a man's anger; she'd only known what she'd seen on TV and in the movies.

"I mean we just met in real life yesterday. This is all happening so fast. I just need time to get settled," she said and kissed his cheek. He looked at her, grabbed her face with both hands and began kissing her. Edna didn't like it. She didn't return his kiss. He reached up her shirt and she tried to push him away. He stopped and looked at her.

"Aw, come on. It'll be nice," he said and pulled her face to his before she could object. She pushed away again, and he pulled her closer. He wrapped his arms around her, and she felt the strength of his hold. Fear welled inside of her. She shut down. She froze. She figured her best option was to not resist. She feared that there was a monster lurking inside of him, just under the surface, but she didn't want to find out. She didn't dare. She went limp and stared at the ceiling, pretending that the rough spackle was a topographical map of a new planet and that she was an astronaut, exploring. He pulled her clothes off, not fazed by her lack of involvement, and she continued to stare at the far away mountains and valleys mapped out above her. The pain was distant and then it was over. She listened to his breathing as it shifted from grunts to the automatic rhythm of sleep. She slowly got up and put her clothes back on.

"Hey," he mumbled into his pillow. "Where are you going?"

"I'm just going to the bathroom," she said.

"Oh," he said. "Will you wrap this in toilet paper and flush it?" he asked as he rolled over and handed her the used condom.

"Um, sure," she said and took it with two fingers and held it away as far away from her as possible. She turned to walk out of the room.

"Hey," he said, propping up on his elbow.

"Yeah," she said, cowering beside the bed.

"Thanks, that was nice."

"Um…"

"Was it good for you? Did you, you know?"

"Um, yeah," she said. "Sure." Her heart folded in on itself like a building being demolished. She knew what had happened was wrong. At least she had survived, and she didn't want to think about it beyond that.

She woke up the next morning, still in the clothes she had traveled in, and thankfully, Shane wasn't in bed next to her. She shut her eyes, wanting to go back to sleep, but the light from the window colored her closed eyelids a bright pink. She wanted to go home.

"Hey sleepyhead," Shane said as he opened the bedroom door with a tray full of breakfast. He sat it down on the sheets next to her. Edna looked at the scrambled eggs, toast, and orange juice. She realized how hungry she was and devoured everything in minutes. "Wow! You're hungry. You want more?" he asked.

"Yes, please," Edna said. She was calmed by the fact that Shane seemed to be in a good mood. *Maybe things'll be different today,* she thought.

"What do you want to do today?" he asked as he brought her another bowl of cheesy scrambled eggs.

"I don't know," Edna said, wondering what there was to do, thinking that she'd honestly just like to go home.

"I'd like to take you downtown Chicago and show you the sights," he said.

"Okay," she said, not knowing how to respond. She was just happy that things had passed from the awfulness of last night into some state of normalness. "I'd like to get a shower before we go. Is that okay?"

"Yeah. Sure. Go ahead."

Edna grabbed her bag and went to the bathroom. She shut the door behind her and tried to lock it, but the button felt loose under her thumb. She began to get undressed. Just as she was stepping into the shower, she heard the door open and saw Shane's mom standing in the doorway. Edna pulled the shower curtain around her and peeked out.

"Jesus Christ," Shane's mom said. "I need to get ready."

"Sorry," Edna said as she hid behind the shower curtain.

"How long are you planning on being here?" she asked.

"I just wanted to wash up. I'll be quick."

"No. How long are you planning on staying in my place?" she asked.

"Mom, mom..." Shane intervened in the hallway. "Relax. We'll be out of your hair in a quick minute."

"How long is *this* girl going to be here? I thought we had an agreement," his mother said. "You know I'm sick of your bullshit, right?"

"Okay, Mom, I get it," Shane said.

"That's what you always say. I'll believe it when I see her gone."

"Mom, you're embarrassing me," Shane said. "Edna's special."

"Special enough to start paying for half of the rent? Special enough to move out? That kind of special?"

"Mom, please don't be like that. Edna is from Minnesota. She's not moving in. She's just visiting," Shane said.

"Humph," his mother said and walked down the hallway.

"Sorry about that, Edna," Shane said as he pulled the door shut.

Edna turned the shower on and adjusted the heat. She stood there, hot water spilling over her back and neck. She was so tense that the water hitting her almost hurt. She let the heat unwind her back muscles. She watched as the water fell from her hair and circled down the drain. She imagined that the spinning water was her tears. She was numb. She couldn't cry. She knew she should be concerned. She knew that her mom wouldn't want her there. She knew that Shane's mom wasn't friendly. She knew that Shane was an asshole. She didn't care. She didn't care because there was no energy left for caring. *Fuck,* she thought.

You're all smart and shit

Shane and Edna climbed on the Metra train. She had never been on a train before, let alone one with two levels. "Can we sit up there?" Edna asked, pointing to the upper deck of the passenger car.

"Sure," Shane said and climbed the narrow stairway to the second level. They sat down in the single row of seats, their backs to the window. Edna twisted around and watched suburb after suburb fly by. "Here," Shane said and handed Edna a beer that he had pulled from a plastic grocery bag he had brought along.

"Um," Edna said, not sure what to do. "We aren't allowed to have these."

"We can drink on the train. People do it all the time," he said.

"Yeah, but we aren't 21," she said, leaning toward him, so no one could hear.

"No one knows that, though," he whispered back to her and smiled. Edna watched him as he opened his can. She expected the other passengers to lift their heads from their phones and newspapers when they heard to crack of the opening beer can, but no one said anything; no one paid any attention to them at all. Edna cracked her beer and sipped it. Her face scrunched up.

Shane laughed. "Is that your first beer?" he asked.

"Yeah," she said, smelling it before taking another sip.

"Well?" he asked.

"I don't really like it," she said, forcing herself to drink another sip.

"It's an acquired taste," Shane said. Edna ended up pretending to drink it and threw the almost full can away before they got off the train.

They took an Uber from the train stop to Michigan Avenue. Chicago amazed Edna. It was so much cooler than she had imagined. The sounds of people and traffic excited her. *I could probably spend all day just people watching,* she thought. They walked to Lake Michigan and then to Grant Park and saw Buckingham Fountain. They stopped at the Bean and took pictures. It reminded Edna of a mirror that she had seen in a fun house at the Minnesota State Fair. She laughed and was surprised that she laughed. *Maybe Shane wasn't such a bad guy,* she thought, and then the memory of what happened the night before lurched into her memory like a monster in a child's pop-up book.

They walked down a path, on a sidewalk that went over a street, to the Art Institute. Shane paid for their admission. "Where'd you get all of the money for today?" she asked, remembering that he took forty dollars from her mom for gas money.

"Don't worry about it," he said and winked at her.

"Have you been here before?" she asked.

"No, but I saw it in a movie once about a kid who skips school with his friends, and it looked interesting, and I thought it'd be a cool place to take you. You're all smart and shit," he said.

They wandered around, neither of them really appreciating the significance of what they were viewing. The ended-up walking down a set of stairs into a room full of miniature rooms. It was called the Thorne Miniature Rooms. The rooms contained dollhouse-size furnishings and were recessed into the wall about a foot and a half. They were at eyelevel and were protected by a pane of glass. It reminded Edna of the shoebox dioramas that she had made in grade school, only these were meticulously crafted and looked real, only small. Edna was enthralled. She felt like she was 12 years old again. She stopped at every display window and stared at the tiny world that it held. There were rooms from different eras and parts of the world, from the frontier days in the United States to various places and eras in Europe. Her imagination ran wild, dreaming that she was a time traveler, traveling to old Europe, looking at the opulent interiors of the tiny rooms. She imagined shrinking and living in those rooms.

Shane had moved through the exhibit faster than she did. He seemed to grow bored with all the art, especially the rooms. Edna didn't mind. She was going to stay as long as she could. With each new display, came a new world to get lost in.

"You ready to go? he asked. "I'd should probably grab a nap before I have to go to work tonight."

"Yeah, sure," she said. The train ride home was painful. She watched scenery that had passed her windows on the way to Chicago, only now it now passed in a reverse order. She imagined that she was watching a film with a happy ending playing in reverse. She was going back to Shane's room, which was, unfortunately, more real than any of the rooms she had seen that afternoon.

I wanna go home

After their trip to Chicago, Edna stayed in Shane's bedroom and slept for three days, only venturing out when Shane and his mother left for work. Her appetite was almost nonexistent. When she did get hungry, she would open the refrigerator door, stare at the containers and baggies that housed the leftovers and would take few bites of this and a sliver of that, hoping that no one would notice, particularly Shane's mom. She feared his mom.

There was a dark sheet hanging over Shane's window, blocking the sun. Edna could tell that the day was gloomy despite the window being covered. Somehow the shadows seeped into the room. She was in bed, staring at the wall when she heard Shane come in; the door slammed behind him. She stared at the wall, hoping that he didn't want anything from her. She shut her eyes, pretending to be asleep.

"Edna," Shane said, shaking her shoulder.

"What?" she asked. "What do you want?" She rolled toward him.

"I'm leaving for work?"

"Okay. And?"

"You ever getting out of bed?"

"I'm just tired," she said, rolling away from him.

"Have you eaten anything?"

"Yes."

"What?" he asked as he sat down on the bed beside her.

"What are you my mother?"

"No," he said, "but you've been acting strange lately. Like you're not the Edna I used to know."

"I eat when you and your mom leave for work. She scares me. I know she doesn't like me. She wants me gone, right?"

"Yeah," Shane said.

"Yeah, what?" Edna asked, rolling over, looking at him.

"Don't take it personally. She's not a happy person," Shane said. "She even hates her boyfriend."

"This sucks. I wanna go home," Edna said and rolled away from Shane again.

"Let me see what I can do to fix this…"

"You mean, take me home?"

"I can fix this and make it better," Shane said. "Trust me."

"Do you have any money?"

"Money? For what?"

"I need some things from the store," she said.

"Just tell me, and I'll grab them on the way home, or we can go together later."

"I can get them myself," she said.

"What do you need?"

"I need tampons," she said.

"Oh," he said, and pulled out his wallet. "Sure. How much do you need?"

"Thirty dollars."

"Thirty dollars? For tampons?"

"I need thirty dollars," she said, staring at him like she hated him.

"Yeah, sure. Here," he said and counted out the cash.

That night, when Shane and his mother left for work, Edna walked to the 24-hour Walgreen's down the street. As she walked, she inhaled the cool evening air, stretched her arms out and twirled around. She smiled. And then she remembered Shane. Her arms fell to her side, and she marched on to the store. She caught a glimpse of her reflection in the cooler glass and did a double take. She was so skinny and even though it was a reflection in a glass door, she could see the dark circles under her eyes. She only recognized the outlines of who she used to be. She saw a ghost of herself staring back. She grabbed tampons, a box of generic sleeping pills, and a cheap bottle of white zinfandel, the cheapest wine there, and took them to the checkout lady.

"ID?" the woman asked just before she ran the wine over the scanner.

"I left it at home," Edna said, patting her pockets.

"Well, I can't sell it you without identification," she said and pointed to the sign: *PHOTO ID REQUIRED FOR PURCHASE OF ALCOHOL.*

"Okay. I'll come back for that," Edna said. The woman set it aside and ran the tampons and the sleeping pills over the scanner.

When Edna got back to the apartment, she went to the bathroom and drew a warm bath. She sat on the toilet, removed the pills from the box, removed the plastic shrink wrap from the bottle top, and pulled the cotton from the inside. *That was a lot of work,* she thought. *I bet Mom would approve.* And with that thought, she remembered their pinky swear. She drained the tub, went to Shane's room, and buried the sleeping pills deep in her bag.

She laid on the mattress and started thinking about her mom. Despite having ignored and deleted recent text messages from her mom and from Jenny, she wondered why she hadn't heard from them in a few days. She went into her contacts to look at her mom's information, because sometimes, just knowing that she was only a call away comforted Edna. Her mother's contact information was gone. It had been deleted. *Shane!* she thought. She then navigated her way to Jenny's info and saw that her contact information had been deleted as well. *I bet he blocked their numbers on my phone, too,* she thought. A flash of what felt like anger passed over her, and she imagined asking Shane about it when he got home. The more she imagined it, the less she felt like asking him about it; the thought of a confrontation fatigued her.

And at that moment, the reflection she had seen of herself in the glass at Walgreens popped into her head, and she was disgusted. *I look hideous,* she thought, and then a parade of unreasonable thoughts marched into her head and took over. *I'm sure they're both doing better without me,* she thought. *I wish I could just die. This is not worth it. Nothing is worth it.* These thoughts played on repeat, over and over again. She curled up on the mattress, hoping to escape, and she did. She fell asleep.

Maybe I am evil

There was this huge, old TV that came with the two-bedroom apartment Joe, his sister, and his mother had moved into after the divorce. The former tenants probably didn't think it was worth moving because it was so heavy, so they left it. The TV came with basic cable, something they had never had before. Joe figured that it must've been hooked up to the homeowner's cable downstairs because he knew that his mother never would've spent the money on cable.

One night, Joe's mother went to drop Jessica off at a friend's house, and he was flipping through the channels, when he stopped because he heard what sounded like people having sex on that channel. The station was scrambled, of course, but he could *hear* the sex, and occasionally, he could see what he thought was a woman's breast flash across the screen. He was aroused, and he didn't pass out like he had in this state before. He was ecstatic.

Just then, his mother came home. She saw him watching the TV, and she heard the sex sounds. Her face knotted with disappointment. The situation quickly killed his new-found happiness. He stood up awkwardly and scrambled to the bathroom. He locked the door. She began knocking.

"We need to talk," she hollered. "This is not what God would want for you. That is disgusting. Impure."

"Mother, please, leave me alone."

"Not until you come out here," she said.

"Please, Mother. I'm sorry." He situated himself, unlocked the door, and slowly walked out.

Revulsion seeped from every expressive part of her face. "And I thought you were from God," she hissed. "I thought you were going to be an important man one day. I thought I was raising a special child, but no. You've fallen from God's grace. You worship your own flesh. You are a sinner. You soul is a wasteland of emptiness."

"Maybe I am evil," he said. She looked terrified, and Joe laughed. Her face twisted dark. Joe laughed even harder, and then he tried to make his laugh sound evil. He saw the disgusted look on his mother's face just before his world went black. He passed out.

The next thing Joe saw was his mother cowering in the corner by the coat closet. Her lip was split and bleeding, and she wouldn't look at him. She stared at the floor. Her hands covered her face as if she were protecting herself. He didn't ask what happened. He scurried into his room and fell onto his bed. *Maybe I am evil,* he thought as he stared at the streetlight just outside his window. *Maybe I am evil...*

Are you praying?

Joe's mother sped down the road in a borrowed, maroon Buick sedan. An old couple from her church had loaned it to her. She suggested that Joe ride in the backseat, so he could sleep. Joe thought it was because he disgusted her. She had arranged for him to spend some quality time with his father, so she was driving him to his new place in Wisconsin. He and Joe were supposed to have a conversation about being a Godly man. Joe suspected that his exile had more to do with the dirty-channel incident than anything.

As they were driving, he became hypnotized by the passing of the plowed rows in the stripped fields that had been relieved of their crops. In the middle of the field, he saw an auburn buck standing under a majestic crown of antlers. The surrounding sky looked dusty to Joe; a brown tinge hung near the edges of the landscape. And the deer stood there in the center of it all, surveying its kingdom. And then Joe saw brown fur explode outward from the deer's shoulder. The blast was red, smoky, and fleshy. The deer tried to run, but its front leg wouldn't move. It wouldn't work. It dragged underneath him. He fell face forward into the rutted earth. The last thing Joe saw out the back window was a burst of dust lit bright by the sunset where the deer had fallen.

"Fuck!" Joe yelled.

"Joseph, you need to stop swearing right this very minute," she said. "Such vulgar words. They come from a decaying mind. You're rotten Joseph Dolsen," she said. Her eyes flashed fear in the rearview mirror.

"I just saw a deer get shot," he said. "There's a deer dying in a field back there."

Her eyes kept vacillating back and forth from the car to the road. She began whispering under her breath. Her words seemed pressured and hurried.

"Are you saying something?" he asked. "Because if you are, I can't understand."

She looked in the mirror and then at the road. Her whispers continued.

"Are you praying?" he asked. She continued to look back and forth. "You're praying, aren't you?" She said nothing and the whispering stopped.

Joe wanted to yell, *Fuck you and your prayers.*

Yes, he became upset, but he realized that he didn't pass out. He just laid down in the backseat and shut his eyes and tried to sleep, but every time he was on the verge of sleep, he'd start grinding his teeth, waking himself up. He knew that he wasn't normal. All he really wanted to be was normal, and as much as he disliked his mother and her religious ways, he hated that she feared him, and she felt the need to pray for protection from him. *That's not normal,* he thought. *I'm not normal.*

It'll solve all of our problems

"Edna," Shane said, kicking the mattress on the floor in his room.

"What?" she asked throwing her arm over her head, speaking into the pillow.

"Come on, get dressed. I've got a surprise for you," he said.

"Can't you just tell me what it is?"

"No. You have to see it," he said. She'd never heard excitement in his voice before. "It'll solve all of our problems."

"Our problems?" Edna asked. "I wasn't aware that we had problems that needed solving," she said as she rolled over and haphazardly pulled on her jeans.

"Never mind that, just come on!"

Shane drove Edna to a pizzeria and didn't park in the main lot but instead parked behind the place.

"This is kinda creepy," Edna said. "You're not going to kill me and put my body in the dumpster, are you?"

"No. Don't be silly," he said. He got out of the car.

"Well, no matter what you say, this is still creepy," she said. She got out and followed him. He walked up the stairs, took a key out of his pocket, and opened the door.

"Ta-da!" he said and opened his arms wide and spun around the empty apartment. "This is our new home!" he said. "We don't have to deal with my mom anymore." He walked into the bedroom. "I bought you this," he said and pointed to a queen-sized bed in the middle of the room on a frame with white posts. Edna went over to examine it. There was a new comforter and new sheets on the bed.

"How did you afford all of this?" she asked.

"I have my ways," he said and smiled. "All we have to do is get our shit from Mom's apartment, and we're in!"

I told you I'd hurt you

That summer, Joe's father got him part-time work weeding a farmer's field. Due to lousy weather conditions, the farmer hadn't been able to spray herbicide when he needed to, so he hired a bunch of high school kids to go through his cornfields and pull out the weeds for him. It was through this job that Joe hooked up with a group of kids his age, and they invited him to a party. His mother never would have approved of these friends. She would've called them sinners and ungodly. Joe's father didn't seem to care what Joe did. He was obsessed with his new girlfriend from church, so Joe went to the party.

When he walked in, he realized that he had never been inside a farmhouse before. He had seen a shit-ton of them from the highway but had never actually been inside one. The plain-white walls were stark with high ceilings. Everything was so simple and crisp and clean. The spotless long lines appealed to him. *God would love the cleanliness of this place,* he thought. He wanted to live there.

There was a lot of drinking that night. Joe drank beer for the first time. He downed one after another and was really loosening up. He actually thought that if he had a chance to get with a girl that night, he'd take it, blackouts be damned. Besides, if he did blackout, who was to say it wasn't because of beer? People did that all the time, right? He knew that the weeding job was done, so he'd probably never see any of these people again, anyway.

With beer coursing through his veins, he began talking to a super-cute girl. Then, out of nowhere, her thick-necked boyfriend walked up to the conversation and just stood there. He was drunk and tried to keep up with the course of the conversation, but he couldn't process the words fast enough. He looked confused; he was consistently one or two beats behind the discourse, looking from the girl to Joe just after either had stopped talking. He must've decided he didn't like what was happening because he wedged his thick-necked self right between Joe and the girl. His face was inches from Joe's. With his every exhale, Joe could feel the warmth of the guy's sour beer breath. The girl snickered. Then, without warning, he shoved Joe into the white wall. Then the boyfriend punched Joe in the mouth and Joe was sprawled out on the floor with blood running from the corner of his mouth. He didn't blackout. It all happened so fast that his beer slogged brain couldn't keep up, couldn't process his emotions fast enough to blackout.

Then Joe felt something snap in the front of his skull. It snapped inside like a piece of celery, and a cooling sensation followed. The cooling was a relief, like it was what was supposed to happen. Only now, somehow, he had left his body and was watching himself from the clean corner of the room near the ceiling.

The next thing he knew, he was back in his body, sitting on the boyfriend's barrel chest, punching him in the face over and over again. "See, I told you I'd hurt you ... I told you this would happen," he said. And then he cried when he saw blood spurting from the guy's nose. "Don't bleed," Joe said, and he tried to push the blood back up in the guy's nose with the palm of his hand. The guy's girlfriend stood, horrified, watching from a safe distance. Little droplets of blood splattered on the white wall. And then Joe left. He ran out the door. He ran all the way back to his father's place. And as he ran, he saw things in the shadows. They moved like whispers, and he heard the soft voices telling him to just get home and go to bed.

I need to know that you're cleansed

After he spent the summer with his father, he was supposed to return to his mother's apartment and continue attending school. There was one thing that his mother wanted him to do before he came back, though. She wanted him to attend a counseling session with her pastor. Joe agreed to one session. It seemed simple enough, and he feared what would happen if he refused.

His mother drove him straight from his father's place to the church. They walked in through the front doors past the large sanctuary. The beauty of the sunlight mesmerized Joe as it blazed through the stained-glass windows. It was magnificent and uplifting. Joe took it as a sign of a new beginning. That, combined with the quietness of the empty church, put his mind at ease. His mother hurried him to the office down the hall.

The pastor was young and lean. He stood up, walked from behind his desk and took Joe's mother's hand in both of his. He asked, "Are you ready?" Joe's mother nodded. "There's nothing to worry about," he said and put his hand on her shoulder. "This is God's will."

"I know," his mother said as she threaded her arm through her purse straps.

"Shall we?" he asked and ushered them out of his office. Joe thought it was strange that the pastor hadn't acknowledge him. He had imagined that there would have been obligatory introductions and then he and Joe would sit in his office and chat. Instead, the pastor had only glanced at him with what Joe interpreted as disgust. Joe followed them into the sanctuary. The pastor climbed the steps at the front of the church and uncovered the baptismal. The blues, greens, and reds of the light shining through the stained glass enveloped him. Joe and his mother were standing at the bottom of the stairs. He turned to them and said, "I'm ready." Joe's mother grabbed his hand with surprising force and pulled him up the stairs toward the pastor.

"What's going on?" Joe asked. The pastor and his mother exchanged knowing glances.

"I need to know that your soul is cleansed before you come back into my home," his mother said. The pastor gave her a nod. There was urgency in his actions as he cupped his hands in the water and then opened them over Joe's head. The water streamed down his face and trickled down the back of his neck. "In the name of the Father, Son and the Holy Spirit," the pastor said, drenching him with holy water three times. Joe shivered and tried to pull away, but the pastor's hands were now on both sides of his face, holding him there. His legs moved back, but Joe couldn't free his head, and then he stopped resisting. He thought about how his mother would interpret his desire to get away from the pastor as evil. He tried to listen as the pastor mumbled something, but he couldn't make it all out because the pastor's hands were over his ears. His mother stood beside him, her arms raised to the vaulted ceiling saying, "Yes God ... Deliver him from the clutches of these demons."

A strange sensation swept over Joe. It was as if bones were humming inside of his body, and, for a moment, he wondered if he had been possessed by demons and now they were all gone. His body was clean, free of evil, ready to go back to his mom's.

Have you seen a dog running around here?

"Still not feeling well?" Joe asked his mother as he walked into the kitchen. There were dishes piled everywhere and empty containers and wrappers laying around, too. It was past noon, and she was still in her bathrobe.

"Nope," she said and grabbed ice cream from the freezer. "The doctor says I've got pneumonia."

"That's not good." He sat down at the table. "You've been sick for a while now," he said as he looked across the small kitchen table. She had gathered a bowl full of ice cream and muskmelon balls.

"I know," she said, dabbing her nose with a tissue. "The doctor said it's going to take a while to get back to normal." And, as if on cue, she had a coughing fit that ended with her hacking something into a tissue. She looked up at him after the fit had passed.

"That's gross," he said, getting up to get some water.

"I'm sorry," she said. "My throat is so raw. The only thing I can eat for relief are these melon balls and ice cream," she said and held up the large spoon. She swallowed it with her eyes shut. "I'm not even hungry." Her speech garbled by ice cream and muskmelon.

"Can I ask you a question?"

"Sure," she said after she swallowed.

"Why didn't you ever take me to see a doctor or a specialist or anything?" he asked.

"What do you mean?"

"My blackouts. Why didn't you ever get me checked out? They might've had medicine to stop them."

"We did. Don't you remember?" she asked.

"I do, but I thought the doctor told us to go see another doctor," he said.

"He wanted you to go see a shrink – a head doctor. There was nothing wrong with you medically," she said. She had a long coughing fit into her bathrobe sleeve. "Besides, your father wouldn't have wanted to spend money on another doctor if nothing was wrong." She coughed again. "We had terrible insurance. There were even times, like between jobs, when we didn't have insurance at all."

"I'm glad you were able to go the doctor for your pneumonia," he said. "I hope you're praying about it, too, because getting hospitalized can get expensive, especially with shitty insurance." He smirked as he drank his water facing the sink, his back to her. He was surprised that his comment hadn't provoked some sort of response from her. He expected an admonishment for swearing at the very least.

He finished his water and still no reply. He assumed that he'd really pissed her off. He turned around, and she looked at him with panic in her eyes. At first, he wasn't sure what to make of it. She started pounding on the table with her open palms, rattling the silverware and the plates on the table. Her face was turning a strange shade of red and then blue, and her drubbing of the table escalated to clenched fists and had become more rapid and fierce. She made the choking symbol with her hands. Joe just stood there. He knew he should do something, but he didn't. Something froze him there. He saw fear in her eyes as she continued pounding the table with closed fists. Her mouth was open as if she were screaming, but no sound came out, only the pounding and rattling of silverware. He watched her eyes.

Oh my God! Oh my God! he thought as a rush of adrenaline coursed through his body. She started stomping and pounding, then the table flipped, and her body landed with a heavy thud on the floor. He stood over her, frozen, paralyzed. She reached for him, and he grabbed her hand and held it. His mind steadied a little at her touch. He knew he should try to dislodge the melon ball from her throat. He knew he should do the Heimlich maneuver. He tried to maneuver her so he could do something, maybe he would do something. He struggled for what seemed like an eternity. Her body went limp, and Joe sat next to her and began to pray, but he wasn't sure what to pray for. He looked at her blank eyes and wondered if she saw him, or if she was gone. "Dear God," he yelled. She stopped moving. He stood up and carefully navigated his way past the chaos on the floor. *What now?* he thought.

He decided it was probably best if he went for a walk and *found* her when he returned. He thought he heard her gasping for breath as he was leaving the house, and just before he pulled the door shut, he stopped, cocked his head, and listened. He heard himself breathing, but not her. *Surely my mind's playing tricks on me,* he thought and pulled the door shut.

He walked around the block to 7-11 and bought a cup of black coffee. He sipped it on his way home, savoring the bitterness. He saw a police car slowly driving toward him, and he panicked. He kept walking, a little faster, reconfiguring the events of the past hour, trying desperately to make everything jive with whatever his mother might have told them if she had rescued herself and called 9-1-1. He was frantically trying to make all the facts work in his favor, or at least make sure he didn't look like a monster who had let his mother die. The police car pulled over to the curb, a sturdy-faced officer waved him over from the sidewalk.

"Hey, what's up?" Joe asked. His empty hand shoved deep into his pocket to keep it from shaking.

"Have you seen a dog running around here?"

"Huh?" he asked, confused.

"A dog? A Husky? You seen one wandering around here?"

"You're looking for a dog?" he asked.

"Yeah. I'm looking for a dog," the cop said, seeming to get a little irritated. "A woman down the street lost her dog, and I'm out looking for it."

"No," he said, trying to fill his voice with respect, "but if I see one running around, I'll call."

"You do that," the officer said, rolled up his window, and drove away.

When he got home, he stuck his head inside the house and called, "Mom."

There was nothing, not a sound. He walked around the lower level and checked in every room downstairs, expecting to see her in one of them. He imagined that she'd be getting cleaned up, or on the phone with the police, or anywhere but on the floor in the kitchen. He couldn't quite bring himself to face his mother lying dead on the floor. After not finding anything, he climbed the stairs of the split level, and, just as his eyes were level with the second floor, he saw her feet in the entryway of the kitchen. One foot was missing a slipper. He could see the pink sock that covered her foot.

He slowly approached. He lost his breath when he saw her body on the linoleum floor. She looked lumpy and lifeless and was on her side in a puddle of melted ice-cream. Her long black hair looked as if it had melded with the ice cream puddle on the floor. He went near, close enough to see the orange of the now liberated melon, resting against her cheek inside her mouth. He grabbed the phone and dialed 9-1-1. As he sat and waited, a confluence of feelings began to swell inside of him, like a wave about to break on the shore. It was sorrow, but in that wave of sorrow was a streak of power. *This must be how God feels,* he thought. He had been the one who decided between life and death, and he had the audacity to choose death. He was high on power. It was unlike anything he had ever experienced in his life.

A strange thought came over him as he sat on the couch in the living room, waiting for the police and ambulance to arrive. He flashed back to that summer morning when he and his mother dipped rhubarb in a sugar bowl on the deck. He remembered how the sour rhubarb had combined with the sweet sugar for an entirely new experience. He smiled at the thought and shivered.

Back to normal

"Edna, get the fuck out of bed," Shane said, pushing the corner of the mattress up, rolling her out the other side. Her hands splayed out to catch herself as she fell to the floor.

"Jesus Christ, Shane," she said. "What the fuck?"

"I'm sick of you laying around all day. All you do is sleep."

"I eat. Maybe if you'd get cable, I'd watch that."

"I rented this place, thinking that you'd get back to normal."

"Normal? What do you mean by normal?"

"You know. The old Edna. The one who used to call me, and we'd talk all night about silly shit. It's like you live in that bed," he said.

"You know why I sleep so much," she asked. Shane shrugged. "I sleep so much because it's the closest I can get to dying without hurting myself."

"Shut the fuck up with that dying shit," he said and waved her off. "You sound crazy."

"Seriously, Shane. I think it's because I don't have my medication. I left it in Minnesota…"

"You don't need medication. Just try to be happier. They say if you smile, and even if it's not a real smile, you will feel happier. It's chemicals 'n shit. Just smile more," he said.

There was a knock at the door. Shane went to open it. Edna listened from the bedroom as the man at the door spoke in hushed tones. "Just calm down," Shane said. "Fine, but next time, don't come here. This is my home. Text me and I'll come to you. Wait here," he said and marched into the bedroom, pulled something out of his backpack, cupping it in the palm of his hand as he passed Edna. He went back to the door and handed the guy whatever he'd pulled out of his backpack. "This'll have to do for now," Shane said. "I'll text you when I get more … Yeah, it'll be soon." He closed the door, went to the refrigerator, and grabbed a beer.

"Do you wanna tell me what that was all about?" Edna asked as she walked out toward Shane.

"It's nothing," he said and opened the beer.

"Nothing? Really? Because it sure looked like a drug deal to me."

"You know what?" he asked and then stopped short.

"What?" Edna asked. "You started. Go ahead – finish – tell me what."

"Yes, it was a drug deal. Yes, I sell drugs. I had honestly stopped selling after rehab and then you…" He stopped and walked to the window.

"Me? I made you start selling drugs again?"

"Yup. This shithole that we're living in – it's owned by the guy I'm dealing for. That bed over there, the one you spend your days in, I bought that with drug money," he said and pointed his beer can toward the bed. "The TV – the PS4 – all bought with drug money."

"So, I'm the reason you're selling drugs again?" Edna asked.

"Yes! Wake the fuck up!" he said and walked over to his backpack, unzipped it and dumped its contents out on the bed. "While you've been sleeping your days away, I've been dealing." Edna saw an electronic scale fall to the bed. She saw a bunch of little baggies, some full, some empty, spill out, and then, as Shane pulled the backpack away from the bed, she saw a gun.

"Is that a real gun?" she asked.

"Yep," he said and picked it up, holding it as if he were weighing it. "Do you want to hold it?" he asked, handing it to Edna. She had never held a gun before.

"No," she said, recoiling. She climbed into bed and pulled the covers tight to her chin. She watched as Shane put everything back into the backpack. Then she heard him playing video games in the next room. Edna's heart raced as she processed everything that he had told her. *I'm living with a drug dealer.* She thought. *I'm sharing an apartment with a man who carries a gun.* She feared Shane before this moment, but now she was terrified of him. *How'd this happen? This is not what I wanted my life to be like at all. Seriously, can my life get any worse?*

When she woke up later that night, Shane wasn't there. She was relieved not to have him around, especially at night. He stole so much from her at night, like blackbirds plucking her soul from her chest one beak full at a time, and now, there was just a black hole at her center. A black hole that pulled her into a dark place where reason was so distorted that she believed that the world would be a better place without her. She got out of bed and retrieved the bottle of sleeping pills from the medicine cabinet in the bathroom. She dumped its contents into her hand and looked at the light blue pills. She wondered if that would be enough to do the job. She went to the kitchen and grabbed one of Shane's beers and opened it. She stared at her hand holding the pills, and saw her little finger, half covered with pills, and she thought of her mom and the pinky swear she'd made with her.

She dumped the beer out in the sink, went back to the bathroom and funneled the pills back into the bottle. She got out her phone and stared dialing her mom's phone number from memory; her finger hovered above the call button, ready to dial, but she couldn't do it. She was so ashamed. What would her mom do anyway? She'd tell her that she should have listened to her, and she hated Shane. *What if she drove down here to get me? What if Mom yelled at Shane? Would he pull the gun on her? What if he was high and angry? Would he shoot her?*

It was then that the irrational thoughts began to parade through her head. *I deserve this,* she thought. *Mom is better off without me,* she thought. *I'm such a piece of shit. I'm a terrible person. I'm tired. I'm so tired. I just don't want to feel anything anymore. That'd be so easy, just ending everything,* she thought. She abandoned the thought of calling her mother and navigated her way to the Women Seeking Men section of Craigslist. Her thumbs moved quickly as she typed up her message and hit enter. She put her phone on do not disturb and went to bed.

Edna and Joe's messages. Back to the beginning.

CRAIGSLIST

Women Seeking Men: I'm an 18-year-old female and I want to take a hit out on myself.

Joe: Hey… Obviously, I'm responding to your ad on Craigslist. WTF? You want to take a hit out on yourself? I'm not saying NO, but I have been depressed and through some shit, too, if you want to talk before you do anything drastic. My name is Joe Dolsen. I'm 20 and not married – not that that matters – just want to help if I can. Email me: joeblackout3117@gmail.com.

Edna: I need help ending my life. I can't do it myself. I need it to look like a murder, so I don't break my mom's heart. I made a promise to her. Can you help?

Joe: I'm not 100% in, but I'm not 100% out either. I may need some convincing. Can you tell me why you want to end your life?

Edna: TBH – I don't even know where to start. I'm so exhausted … I don't think I have the energy to go over everything. I'll try……

My "boyfriend" is abusive.

He raped me.

He sells drugs.

The world would be a better place without me.

I just want to be done. I see no point to going on. None.

I'm exhausted. I need to be done.

I don't want to live any more.

You're just going to have to trust me. I'm a … I don't feel like I should have to explain this to a stranger. Either you can help or you can't. I'll pay you. If you can find it in your heart to help me just send me a day and time that you can pick me up in Elk Grove. I prefer that it be at night because that's when he works. Please don't mess with me. Only do this if you're serious. 100%.

Joe: You seem like you're in a bad spot, and that troubles me. How about we correspond for a bit, and then, if I can help you, I will? If not, well, we'll deal with that if it happens. Meanwhile, if someone else takes you up on your offer, feel free. But please let me know, so I don't spend eternity wondering what happened to you. Can you send me a picture?

Edna: A pic? Fuck you.

Joe: I guess I don't need a pic.

Edna: Fine. Right now, you're my only option. My only hope. Please!

Joe: I've had a pretty fucked up life, so I get it.

Edna: I guess you could say I've lived a fucked up life, too.

Joe: What do you do for a living?

Edna: Nothing. Basically I'm being held hostage by my "boyfriend"!

Joe: Really? Do you want me to call the police?

Edna: NO! PLEASE! Don't call the cops. I don't think that would be good. They wouldn't do anything anyway and that would piss off Shane and the last thing I need is Shane pissed off.

Joe: Fine. Your choice.

Edna: Why did you answer my ad anyway?

Joe: TBH, your ad was just too intriguing to pass up. I was sooo curious. I had to respond.

Edna: Please don't fuck with me. This isn't a game.

Joe: I'm not fucking with you. This might sound strange, but I think killing you is a real possibility for me. I'm not sure why. Part of me not saying YES right away is because I need to sort through this all myself. It's strange that I'd say YES, but at the same time, I'm thrilled by the thought.

Edna: Thrilled? Please take this seriously. Don't just get your rocks off.

Joe: ...?

Edna: Okay. Whatever works for you. Just please......

Joe: We'd need some sort of agreement that it was an assisted suicide or something like that, you know, so I don't get in trouble with the law. Maybe an informal contract?

Edna: You're screwing with me? Yes?

Joe: ...?

Edna: We could work up a contract. Wouldn't these messages work? Just show the police these.

Joe: Yeah. This correspondence would probably work. For the record, I'm serious. I think we ... I could get away with it. Besides, I don't think jail would be that bad. I'd get three squares a day and plenty of downtime to read and maybe time to write a novel.

Joe: Also, I've heard that experiencing an ending of life with someone is one of the most intimate things someone could do... Is any of this scaring you off?

Edna: It's weird. You're weird, but I don't care. I just want to be done with everything. I'm going to keep sifting through the responses from the ad. There were a lot of guys but most of them were really really creepy.

Joe: I understand. Please keep in touch. Let me know if you find anyone or not.

Edna: Sure.

Are you ready to kill me?

Joe: Hey, how are you doing?

Edna: Are you ready to kill me?

Joe: I'm still NOT saying no. I take it you haven't had any luck with anyone else?

Edna: I emailed a dude back and we were supposed to meet at a gas station somewhere public you know and I saw him and got a bad vibe. I know I'm going to be dead and everything but ... I don't want my body to disappear forever. So, I kept on walking.

Joe: It's almost like you need a service to sort through all the applicants. Am I right?

Edna: Ugh not funny. Please, please help me. The only reason I'm getting out of bed every day is to check my email to see if you've decided to kill me.

Joe: I've been thinking about the whole thing A LOT and there have been more days that I could do it than there are days that I could not.

I'm not trying to save you

Joe: You there? You still around?

Edna: I haven't offed myself yet if that's what you're asking.

Joe: I'm honestly relieved that you're still around. I was concerned because I hadn't heard from you.

Edna: Yeah.

Joe: …how are you?

Edna: I hope you're not trying to save me.

Joe: What do you mean?

Edna: This whole thing is dragging out waaay too looong.

Joe: No, I'm not trying to save you. I promise

Edna: Have you ever used a gun?

Joe: I have, as a matter of fact.

Edna: Have you ever killed someone?

Joe: No, but I watched my mother die. I let her die…

Edna: Let here die?

Joe: Yes. It's a long story.

Edna: I'm going back to bed. Please don't email me unless you're willing to shoot me. I can a gun, and I can get some cash, but you've gotta be 100% in before I sell what I need to sell to get the cash, because there's no going back after that. I am exhausted, Joe. I'm done. Do you get it?

Joe: I get it.

Edna: Goodbye Joe.

I guess I don't know you

Joe: Edna … are you there?

Edna: I'm here. Why? Are you ready?

Joe: Can you send me a picture?

Edna: No.

Joe: I just think seeing you will help me make up my mind.

Edna: No need for a picture. Pretty sure I've got someone who will kill me. I just need to get him the drugs he wants and then figure out a time that works. Thanks for even considering this though. I know it must have been hard on you dealing with such a messed up person and all…

Joe: I wouldn't say that at all. I've enjoyed getting to know you.

Edna: Huh? You don't *know* me.

Joe: Yeah. You're right. I guess I don't know you. I just feel close to you for some reason. I feel connected to you somehow. Sorry. This whole thing is strange.

Edna: Thanks for considering it Joe. I know it was a big ask.

Joe: What if I said I'd do it? I've given it a lot of thought, and I'm pretty sure I could do it. I don't want some other guy to pull the trigger. I feel like that's my job.

Edna: I feel like you're the type of guy who'd get all stupid when it came right down to it. You'd tell me you loved me or some shit like that and try to get me to run away with you.

Honestly I have no energy for that sort of bullshit. I don't wanna to deal with any shit. You know? If you pulled something crazy like that, I'd kill you and I'd then kill me. Got it? This is taking too much of my time. I'm exhausted. Will you please just kill me already? Promise me that's what you'll do?

Joe: Yes. Name the place and time and I'll be there.

Edna: Fine. This Thursday @ 10PM @ Thorton's Gas station in Elk Grove. Don't bother showing up if you're not going to go through with it. Once I've committed to this either you're killing me or I'm going to kill myself. So do it for my mom who doesn't want her daughter to commit suicide if nothing else. I promised her I wouldn't do it. Help me keep that promise.

Joe: I will. I'll be there.

I'd be more comfortable not being here

The gas station pavilion was lit up like a lighthouse in the darkness. Joe parked his old Honda Civic in front and waited in his car. He looked over his shoulder and then at his phone for the time: 9:56 p.m. He got out and shut the door. He stood frozen with fear beside his car, his hand, shaking, still on the door handle. He heard the buzzing of the fluorescent lights overhead. Fear flooded his brain, and panic spread like spilt water across a tile floor. *What if this is an elaborate setup by the police? What if some teenagers are pranking me and filming it for their YouTube channel? What if her boyfriend shows up and tries to kill me?*

He decided to wait in the store where he was less exposed. He stood in the candy aisle and looked over the fixture at the parking lot outside. He saw a young woman wearing a backpack, walking out of the shadows and turning toward the gas station. She had on shorts and her hands were tucked into the front pocket of her gray hoodie. Joe looked at his watch: 10:00. He walked out to his car.

"Edna?" he asked as she got closer.

"Joe?" She adjusted the backpack.

"Yeah..."

"Is this your car?"

"Yeah."

"Can we get in and drive? I'd be more comfortable not being here. It's too close to the apartment."

"Of course. Get in," Joe said and hurried into the car. He reached over popped open the passenger's side door. She took off the backpack.

"Can I set this in the back seat?"

"Oh, yeah. Sure," he said. She opened the back door and set the backpack on the seat, shut the door and climbed in. "Where to?" he asked.

"I was thinking that Busse Woods would be a good place to do this. It's so big. The only problem is that the gates to the park are locked at sunset. We could drive into the neighborhoods around the woods, find a place to park, and walk into it. I've got the gun and the PS4 in the backpack. Have you ever used a handgun before?" she asked.

"Not a handgun, but I'm sure it's not too different than a rifle," he said. His hands were sweaty on the steering wheel.

"Look there," she said, "it's a pawn shop," she pointed as they drove past. Do you wanna stop and trade the PS 4 in for cash now? It might be easier with me now than after it's all over?"

"Sure," Joe said, happy for the distraction. He turned around and they pulled into the pawn shop.

While Edna went inside to pawn the PS4, Joe sat in his Honda and thought about what the night had in store. Deep down, he knew that wanting to help Edna kill herself was partially about the rush that he had experienced when his mother died. He wanted to feel that again.

He also knew that her death would be an intimate act; maybe even the most intimate thing that two people could ever share. He had never experienced anything this emotionally charged, and he knew it was strange, but he was looking forward to sharing the end of Edna's life with her. While he didn't love Edna, he loved the idea of helping her out. He loved the idea of being her savior. It was then and there that he knew for sure that he would kill Edna for free if she came out of the pawn shop without any money.

There's no going back

"Two-hundred-dollars," Edna said as she got in the car. "I didn't think it'd be worth that much."

"Yeah, they're twice that new," Joe said as he started the car. "Well, where do you wanna to go?"

"Let's duck into that neighborhood, park the car, and then walk into the preserve," she said, pointing across the street.

"Are you sure you want to do this?" he asked.

"There's no going back, now," she said. "I'm putting the money in my back pocket. You can get it when it's all over. Fair enough?" she said, leaning forward in her seat.

"Sure," Joe said.

"You can have Shane's gun, too. You might not wanna to sell it to a pawn shop or somewhere legit, but you could probably get some more money for it, you know."

"Okay," Joe said, half listening to what she was saying.

"Here. Park here," she said. Joe parked. She got out of the car and grabbed the backpack from the backseat. "Let's go," she said and began walking. Joe followed her. They walked down the street to the stoplight and crossed when no cars were in sight. They walked past the closed gate and down the bike path.

"You know, this would be a lovely walk if we weren't going to do what we're going to do." Joe said. "The moonlight lighting up the bike path. The frogs croaking and the light summer breeze. It'd be absolutely beautiful if you didn't want to be killed."

"Yeah. That's funny. You need to do this. *We* need to do this. I'm all in now. I've sold the PS4. There's no going back to Shane," she said and walked down the path ahead of Joe. "This looks good." She turned and pointed to the little dirt path off to the side. "This path looks like it doesn't get used a lot. It'll be perfect. You'll have plenty of time to get out of here and get rid of your clothes, or whatever you need to do."

"I hadn't thought of that," Joe said. Edna walked off the trail onto a divergent dirt path. Joe followed silently.

"Here," she said. "I'll get on my knees here, and you'll shoot me in the back of the head."

"Execution style," Joe said.

"What?"

"It's called execution style," he said.

"Oh," Edna said. "I wouldn't know."

"I saw it in a mob movie," he said.

"Okay," Edna said as she unzipped the backpack and pulled out the gun. "Take this." She handed him the gun.

The weight of the gun was considerable in his hands. His arms trembled with anticipation. "Can we pray about this before we do it?" he asked. "I'm not usually one for prayer, but just in case, you know?"

“Yeah. I’d like that,” she said. She fell to her knees. Joe got on his knees beside her, set the gun down, and pressed his hands together. Edna did the same.

“Dear Lord,” Joe began. “Please, if you don’t want us to do this, give us a sign now. If this is in your plans, please forgive us for what we are about to do. Amen.”

“Amen,” Edna said. Joe grabbed the gun and stood up. Edna remained on her knees. “Okay. Let’s do this, Joe!” she said, her voice loud in the woods.

“Okay. You’re sure?”

“As I’ll ever be. I’m at peace with this,” she said.

Joe looked to the heavens, switched off the safety, and pointed the gun at the back of Edna’s head. And then…

Joe blacked out.

Joe and Edna and the Hollywood ending

Joe was on his belly when he came to; his cheek pressed into pine needles, and he was confused. Slowly, it all came back to him. He jumped up and looked for Edna's body. He saw nothing. He examined the ground for blood or an empty bullet cartridge or for some sign of what had happened. Again, nothing.

"Edna. Edna," he whispered. "Are you here?"

Nothing. He groggily walked back to the bike path, looking for signs of Edna the whole way. He tried to figure out how long he'd been unconscious. He noticed that the moon now seemed smaller, and the frogs had stopped croaking.

He went back along the bike path, crossed the road, and tried to walk as nonchalantly as he could through the neighborhood where they had parked his car; it wasn't there. He looked around for towing signs, but there were none. He patted his pant pockets for his keys. They were gone. He instinctively reached around to his back pocket for his wallet. It was gone, too. "No! No! No. No," Joe said as he shook his fists at the moon.

Edna's Hollywood ending continued

Edna got in Joe's car and adjusted the seat. She adjusted the rearview mirror and started the engine. She drove to a gas station, filled up the tank, bought three bottles of Mountain Dew, and a road atlas. She knew she could navigate home using her phone, but it scared her. She wasn't sure that she wanted to deal with messages from Joe or from Shane. She wanted time to process things.

"We don't sell too many of those anymore," the cashier said, pointing to the atlas. "You know with technology and everything,"

"I imagine you don't," Edna said. She got back in Joe's car, turned on the dome light, flipped open the atlas, and found the best route back home to Norwood. She was worried about what her mom would say and not sure what she'd tell her. She realized that she had a seven-hour ride home to figure it all out.

Joe and Edna and what (probably) really happened

*Reader beware: If you liked the Hollywood ending, you had best stop reading here. DO NOT CONTINUE!

Joe was on his belly when he came to. His cheek pressed into pine needles, and he was confused. Then it all came back to him. He turned his head and saw Edna's pale face staring at him; the glow of the moon reflected in her blunted eyes. He noticed that a quarter of her skull had exploded outward just above her right eye. He wondered if he was dreaming. He pulled himself up to a sitting position and questioned whether he'd pulled the trigger, or if she'd pulled it after he'd blacked out. He brought his right hand to his face and could smell the scent of gunpowder all over his hand. He looked around and found the gun near where he had regained consciousness.

He picked the gun up from the forest floor covered with long pine needles and walked to the dam further down the bike path. He stood on the bridge and threw the gun as far as he could. He heard the splash and watched the ripples catch the moonlight as they floated outward. He went back to Edna, got the $200 from her back pocket and walked out of the woods.

Joe called in sick for the next three days. It was on the third day that the police knocked on his door.

"Joe Dolsen?" The young officer standing at his door asked.

"Yes sir," he said respectfully.

"We've got some questions for you. We were wondering if you'd be willing to come down to the station with us and have a chat?"

"I thought you might be by," he said and walked to the squad car with the officer.

About the Author

Jason Fisk lives and writes in the suburbs of Chicago. He has worked in a psychiatric unit, labored in a cabinet factory, and mixed cement for a bricklayer. He currently teaches language arts to eighth graders. He was born in Ohio, raised in Minnesota, and has spent the last few decades in the Chicago area. He recently had a collection of poetry published by Kelsay Books: *Sub Urbane.* He also had a number of books and chapbooks published: *Sadly Beautiful*, essays, poems, and short stories published by Leaf Garden Press; *Salt Creek Anthology,* a collection of micro-fiction published by Chicago Center for Literature and Photography; *the fierce crackle of fragile wings,* a collection of poetry published by Six Gallery Press; and two poetry chapbooks: *The Sagging: Spirits and Skin,* and *Decay,* both published by Propaganda Press.